FALSE PROPHET

A NOVEL

BY DAVE JEFFERY

DAVE JEFFERY
FALSE PROPHET

EERIE RIVER PUBLISHING
www. EerieRiverPublishing.com

Paperback ISBN: 978-1-998112-47-0

Edited by Erika Mendelson
Cover Artwork Justicia Satria, @barokahstudio24
Cover Design Michelle River of Eerie River Publishing
Book Formatting by Michelle River of Eerie River Publishing

ALSO BY DAVE JEFFERY

THE 'A QUIET APOCALYPSE' SERIES

A QUIET APOCALYPSE
CATHEDRAL
THE SAMARITAN
TRIBUNAL
MONUMENT: THE 'A QUIET APOCALYPSE' OMNIBUS

THE BEATRICE BEECHAM SERIES

FEARSOME FEAST
FETE OF FATE
HOUSEFUL OF HORRORS
CRYPTIC CRYPT
SHIP OF SHADOWS
THE DEVIL DEVICE

THE FROSTBITE TRILOGY

FROSTBITE
LABYRINTH
EARTHFALL

COLLECTIONS

MOOD SWINGS
SCREAMS & WHISPERS

CHAPTER ONE

"Look into my heart and you will see only darkness. I am the void. I am the *abyss*."

Detective Inspector Malcolm Cross stared at the dishevelled figure sitting opposite. Two men, separated by a wooden interview table, and an irrepressible fog of doubt. The man across the table was Raymond Tonks. He wore a crumpled, white anti-rip overall, a thick, red wheal smiling from his throat. Whiskers shadowed Ray's squared jaw, and his glasses were jammed onto the bridge of his nose—rigid, as though the frames were nailed there. Cross observed the small circular indent over Tonks' right eye and was tempted to ask how he'd got it, but far more important matters were pressing.

The two-way conversation was being watched from behind one-way glass. The mirrored pane reflected magnolia walls that blanched under the fluorescent lights, making the interview room as insipid as the cheese sandwiches the detective had brought with him from the station cafeteria. The sandwiches were now lying on the table, a transparent plastic pyramid in no man's land.

"Well, we can explore what you mean by that in due course, Mr Tonks," Cross said as he pushed the sandwiches forward. The carton squeaked as it made the journey to Tonks' side of the table. "Is it okay if I call you Raymond?"

"Ray is better."

"Ray it is," Cross confirmed. "I'm Detective Inspector Malcolm Cross. Please call me Malcolm."

"Malcolm," Ray whispered as though testing it out.

Cross responded with a warm smile. "Try to eat. We're going to be here for a while."

Ray acknowledged neither the amity, nor the sandwich. Instead, he fumbled with his wrist, seemingly twisting the winding mechanism of a watch that had been seized and sent to a forensics lab in Birmingham. The action appeared as though he was trying to turn back time, yet was destined to relive this bleak moment forever.

Cross flicked a finger upon his electronic tablet. "I understand that you've waived your right to legal representation?" The shimmering light from the screen made his eyes sparkle like black ice on a winter road.

"That's right," Ray said, still playing with his wrist. He rubbed his fingers together, reminding Cross of someone rolling dry snot. People working with dementia sufferers called it 'pill rolling'. The detective knew this because Alzheimer's disease had robbed him of his father eight years ago. He could sometimes still hear his father's terrified screams in the night. The memory came unbidden, and Cross pushed away the heavy shadow of melancholy that came with it.

"I guess I'm obligated to tell you to reconsider."

"I won't change my mind."

The detective let the silence roll out. It was his ally at such times. There was no pressure—he had to give Ray time to stew, consider his next move. It was *technique*, carefully presented with a side of experience. People were different, and their responses to an interview were equally so. Some preferred soft soap, others the more direct approach, but the fundamentals were always the same; he knew them all too well.

Everyone talks in the end, he thought. *Be that through the skill of the interviewer, the relief of unloading guilt, the hope of cutting a deal for a reduced sentence, or the arrogance of displaying criminal achievement.*

Everyone talks.

Cross patted an oblong, twin-tape recorder. Its bulky, black carcass had front-loading trays, and two buttons—one grey and one red.

"Obviously, I have to record this interview. And it's also being captured on video via that camera in the corner of the room." He pointed at the camera—small, but still conspicuous.

Ray paid no attention to either. "Record what you want. No one ever believes me. Why should you?"

"I'm paid by the hour. That means my mind is forever open. Something *truly* horrific has happened this evening. I'm just interested in *your* perspective on things."

Cross activated the cassette recorder, making his official introductory statement with the kind of smoothness that experience brings to the table. Once he'd concluded, he settled back in his seat. "Over to you, Ray."

Ray began talking almost immediately. "The mind is an incredible thing when one keeps it open. Some would say it can also be a terrible thing." Ray smirked as he looked down at the sandwiches. He stopped playing with the imaginary watch on his wrist. He looked up, and in those eyes, Cross saw a man, haunted. Sullen sockets, smudged dark by lack of sleep, played host to bright blue irises dulled by fatigue.

"When you say 'some', do you mean *you*?" Cross asked.

"Maybe. So ..."

"So *what*?"

"So, where shall I start?" Ray whispered in an inquisitive tone. It was rhetoric. "The day of the earthquake seems as good a place as any."

"The earthquake?"

"Yes, the one in Indonesia. An 8.7. 800,000 dead."

"Okay," Cross said. "It's your show. Let's light it up."

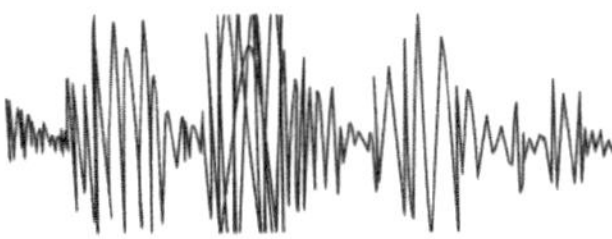

The floor space about him is filled with desks laid out in neat rows, with hi-spec PCs splashing blue light on the faces of the many people judiciously typing away on their keyboards. Others are scrolling with wireless mice. The workforce all wear blue blazers and the panther motif—sewn into the breast pocket with golden thread—is replicated on the far wall of this place of glass and chrome, signifying the company tradition for strength and loyalty.

Like the colleagues around him, he is also sat at his desk. His computer shows an animation he's working on, an engine turbine rotating lazily in 3D. His cursor prods and probes, making minor amendments on the graphic that ultimately mean big changes in the world of aerospace. Once he has finished, his hands go to the cup of Sulawesi coffee, and he takes a sip. The sweet taste revives him instantly.

As he takes in his drink, he looks up. The window ahead is made of plate-glass, and gives way to an incredible view of the Jakarta Utara harbour district. Beyond that is the Indonesian seascape where the Java Sea is a blue streak through the city smog.

Jakarta is sinking—thirteen feet in the past forty years. The seawall, known locally as 'Great Garuda', was erected as a line of vertical cylinders to combat regular floods during monsoon season. It is a stark reminder of just how vulnerable they all are to the whims of nature.

He knows their city may be the Indonesian capital, but the island of Java where it resides is on fragile footing. Indonesia sits in the 'Pacific Ring of Fire', with 452 active volcanoes in the region. Minor seismographic incidents are commonplace. Mainly they are small and inconsequential, but he is under no illusion as to the ferocity these lands can elicit. The country has seen some of the most devastating earthquakes and volcanic eruptions in history.

In 1883, the island of Krakatau in the Sunda Strait didn't erupt, it exploded, killing over 37,000 people, an estimate that he knows is conservative at best. The blast could be heard three thousand miles away. His grandfather told tales, handed down through generations; stories of family members who had witnessed the event being left blind by the intense light the blast gave out. The truth behind such claims may have been suspect, but the devastation is without dispute.

In 2004, Sumatra—in the western part of the country—saw up to 280,000 people killed in a tsunami after a seaquake. In 2017 alone, the city of Jakarta incurred nineteen earthquakes, with several deaths. But seismologists were predicting an 8.7 event over the next few years, a quake that was feared would level the city.

Although incongruent, he smiles at such a claim. How could one live a life in such fear? The local population just carried on regardless, used to living with the constant threat. Yes, the ground would shake from time to time, but a repeat of the 2004 tsunami was not likely to happen in his lifetime.

This conclusion is still fresh in his mind as he goes to place his coffee on his desk. The room lurches to the right. The mug misses the table and goes to the floor, shattering in a tiny ceramic explosion. There is a sudden noise in the room—the grinding roar of protesting metal and concrete, and the terrified screams of all those about him.

The offices begin to oscillate, the tables and chairs, the people— all juddering. The whole structure shifts to the left, and everything goes with it. He is hit by flying debris, and a VDU strikes him in the sternum. He feels something give. Breath knocked from him, he reels towards the windows, slamming into one of the panes that is as hard as hitting a pavement. His vision blurs with blood, but not before he is able to see the devastation below.

The whole world is a writhing sea of destruction. The roads and infrastructure are crumbling as the ground rolls like a sheet aired in the wind. There are explosions as gas mains crack and ignite under the onslaught, the flames blossoming skywards. Some of the burning debris look like people.

Something smashes into the window next to him. It is the severed head of one of his work colleagues, a man with a son who has gone to work for Rolls-Royce in Singapore. The man was so proud when he'd spoken of it, but now all his mouth can do is twitch like it has forgotten its purpose.

The air is suddenly filled with a terrible screech, and one half of the ceiling collapses, the building folding in on itself. People tumble like rag dolls, bodies made shapeless as they pass through the imploding infrastructure, a vile red mist marking their passage.

The building lists back to the right, and the windows suddenly creak and crack as their frames dislocate. Then the whole mezzanine is filled with glass splinters as each pane pops. The window against which he leans disintegrates, shredding him, blinding him, but the great howling wind that forces itself past him defines his last moments. He is sent backwards and becomes one with the crumbling building.

Below him, the city of Jakarta trembles as fires blaze and huge trenches gape. The tower building topples like a tree felled by a woodsman's axe, the great cloud marking its landing lost amongst the catastrophic maelstrom on the ground.

Then the earthquake stops, and there is a pause in the destruction. Tiny cries and screams rise through the moans of dying buildings. But it is a mere respite. The steady roar returns. This time it is not the land that has a voice, but the ocean. The tsunami is forty feet high and rolls in from the Java Bay. And like an insatiable, ravenous animal, it eats everything in its path.

CHAPTER TWO

Ray woke up, his heart pounding against his sternum, the organ seemingly bored of being cooped up and seeking escape. His body was moist, the duvet damp and unpleasant. The pungent scent of stale sweat brought him round like smelling salts.

All about him, the bedroom was quiet, the light seeping in through the window blinds carrying a muted tone. Instinctively, he pawed at his face and sought out his mobile phone on his bedside cupboard. Once in his sweat-slick palm, his iPhone told him it was six in the morning. The empty space beside him proved his wife was already up.

"Fuck. This is early, even for you, Denise," he muttered to the gloom.

Ever since they'd first met, his wife of twenty-five years had a penchant for an early morning run. Over the passing years, her propensity for distance appeared to extend to their relationship.

He didn't blame her. Time was sometimes a thief when maintaining relationships, and he'd been guilty of aiding and abetting on more than a few occasions. Some may have called it complacency, while others saw it as familiarity. He just called it *life*, and in its sway the finer points of a marriage had been chipped away until all that remained was blunt reality.

He played with the idea that, perhaps, his wife had disturbed him as she'd got ready to put in her ten-kilometre jaunt. But he knew the real reason why he was awake at this god-awful hour, in a bed that was so wet he could've pissed in it for all anyone knew.

Sitting up, he found the edge of the mattress and hunched, elbows on knees, a palm against his greasy forehead.

Sometimes there was no hiding the reason. He'd tried that before and almost ended up—

"Not now, Ray," he whispered to the room. "Not *now*, damn it."

He'd been dreaming again. Awareness had robbed him of clarity, his dreams scuttling for cover like rats in a torch beam. Yet, whilst the details had become ghosts, their essence remained. Like disquiet thoughts after terrible news.

He remembered looking down on a shivering landscape, the ground undulating as though fluid, waves of rock and tarmac washing against the skyscrapers that fought to stay upright in the onslaught. The dream lasted only seconds longer than the quake, but in that time, the destruction was total.

And real.

The comic books called it precognition. The scientists called it a myth. Parapsychology blamed primordial instincts, long since redundant in the world of technology. Psychology blamed the subconscious fantasies of a fractured mind in societal meltdown.

No matter how others chose to frame it, ever since the day at school where he'd managed to blend youth and idiocy in a single moment of madness, Ray *had* it, owned it, and lived it. Absently, he rubbed at the indent over his right eye, a reminder of how all of this started.

His mind pulled up short. No going back to what *had* happened, just what was happening right now. Or, more to the point, what was *about* to happen.

Terrible events that Ray had seen, and always just before they occurred. No time to do anything about them.

Ever.

And the one time he did try, his parents just gave him a condescending chat about *The Boy Who Cried Wolf*, followed up with threats to take him to see a child psychiatrist. Back then it was bad enough to have had an accident born from folly, let alone being branded 'mad'. School wasn't the place to have such labels. Not then, not now.

So, he suffered in silence. But it was others who paid the price.

The guilt didn't help. Nuzzling against him and keeping his company through college and university.

After that, there was Denise. Ray had no desire to impart his abilities to his wife-to-be. Instead, there was just a bold lie to smooth the edges. He called them his 'blackouts'. Later, at her insistence, he feigned hospital appointments and MRI scans, and came back with a diagnosis of *absence seizures*, a form of epilepsy in which people wink out rather than have a fit. In truth, he hadn't got this diagnosis from a qualified neurologist, but rather an afternoon of research on Google Scholar. It was convincing enough for his wife, seeing as they both worked in healthcare. Plus, he'd had two decades to say the words enough to make them sound real.

But never to himself.

Because when he did start to believe his visions were part of a brain dysfunction that medics had given a thousand and one names, the images and events would strike him down without warning, a little psychic reminder that the curse was still along with him on his life's journey.

And the dream of the quake had been one such reminder. As he wandered into the bathroom to shower, Ray consoled himself with the notion that at least this particular vision had been dulled by sleep.

He closed the shower door and let the hot water blast away the last vestiges of memory, the steam fogging any lingering thoughts. It was working well, to the point where he was about to count himself lucky for the first time in what seemed like a lifetime.

Then, as it usually did, a searing bolt of pain ripped through his brain, and the world *changed*.

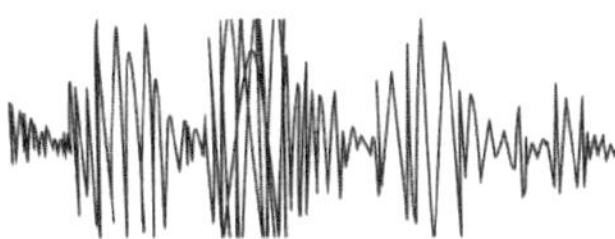

Denise's feet pounded the asphalt, her breathing and footfalls in perfect rhythm with the beat of The Human League's *DARE!* album coming through her headphones. Between her shoulder blades, a large teardrop of sweat seeped through her tee-shirt, her legs—bare below her mid-thigh length Lycra shorts— cool and slick as they cut through the air. Her hair, usually in a grey shoulder-length bob, was pinned away from her face by tortoiseshell clips. Intense brown eyes surveyed the lane ahead.

The Worcestershire countryside was sedate, yet alive; early enough for the wildlife to still lay claim to the landscape. She'd already seen three rabbits, a deer, and a skulking fox on her route through the rural areas surrounding their village. The narrow country lanes, even with their skeletal, autumnal hedgerows and trees, were perfect for harbour and protection, the animals taking advantage of them as they saw her approach. Only the fox stopped for a few seconds, regarding her with a nonchalant air that made her smile. In half an hour or so these creatures would be nowhere to be seen as cars, cutting through from Bromsgrove town on their way to the nearby M42, would skim through the lanes, going far too fast—getting to work on time was the only focus of their impatient drivers.

Despite this, she preferred braving the lanes, even with their long stretches without any pavements, where a runner was at the mercy of petrol heads or those not familiar with the etiquette of driving on country roads. She'd tried a running machine, and it had its value, especially in the winter months where running at night on roads such as this was tantamount to Russian roulette. Locally, three people had been seriously injured when cars had collided with them on dark bends, even with high-visibility tabards and head-torches in situ.

A slight incline had her quickening her pace; the purple *Fitbit* on her wrist had laid down a challenge to bring this all home in less than fifty-five minutes. The thought of home triggered images of her sleeping husband.

Ray had been particularly restless in bed last night—dreaming again, no doubt. A few elbow nudges had quietened him for a while, but it wasn't long before he was fidgeting once more. Eventually, she'd decided it was time to get up and leave him to it. Going out on her run earlier was never going to be a chore. She loved this time of the morning; it gave her a sense of peace that eluded her for most of her day.

The job she'd held for over a quarter of a century made demands that left little of her resolve. What remained at the end of each day was the need to offload, an outpouring of emotion and frustration that came with working in the National Health Service (NHS). Her husband was adept at pretending to listen; more often than not he did take in enough to offer guidance. His own experience working in healthcare was enough to make any suggestions both timely and useful.

After all their years of marriage, many would have considered themselves lucky that their partner even pretended to listen. This was certainly the case when she took note of the gripes from her work colleagues. They would often talk about how they felt invisible when they got home, and she listened to their woes and, with the occasional pang of guilt, took comfort from their ills.

She and Ray had a routine, and it was something that she never thought she'd come to appreciate. In her younger days, she'd recoiled at the thought of schedules, preferring to have a more flexible approach to the day. This put her firmly in contention with school, of course. Her parents had forever been sitting her down to discuss the 'school rules', and in this she only ever saw the rhetoric of the teaching staff, and rebelled in any way she could.

Repercussions for her behaviours were, however, token. The main issue was that while Denise refused to follow rules that she saw as inconsistent and petty, she would still produce the grades and, as frustrating as this was for the teachers, it was always enough to avoid serious sanction.

A rebel *with* a cause, after all.

These days, she *needed* routine; it had influence, no matter how much she disliked it. Most of the time, she swallowed it, took it for what it was—a necessary evil to maintain a busy work schedule. But sometimes the old contentions would arise, and she'd feel the teenage mutineer rising to the surface.

It had happened far too many times recently. The events flitted through her mind, and they came with a blend of intense excitement and bitter remorse.

She tried to power through it but guilt generated a sharp stab of concentrated emotion that swelled in her chest, leaving her stomach hollow and her mouth watery despite the exertion. It had her slowing and then suddenly pulling up, hands on hips, her breathing heavy now that she had lost control.

She heard the car before she saw it, wiping the tears of exertion from her eyes as she looked up. Her breathing stalled as she saw the familiar red VW Beetle coming towards her. The driver's window slid down as it pulled up alongside her.

Panicked, she shook her head and pulled her face into a frown. "You can't be here," she said, her voice terse. "We had an agreement."

The driver smiled and it was warm and beautiful, making the guilt brighter. "What we have is *intense*. Remember what you said? You said it's the first time you've felt alive in years."

Denise sighed heavily. "We've discussed this already. What we were doing was wrong. A mistake."

The driver rummaged in the footwell and brought up a gift. "*Several* wonderful mistakes, as I recall. Perhaps we could make another soon?"

She was presented with a flat, square box. Her frustration at being ignored was made clear by the cold stare Denise returned. She made no attempt to take what was on offer.

"I chose it especially for you," the driver said. "It's your favourite. You told me it made you feel out of control. You remember saying that? When we made our *mistakes*?"

Denise snorted in anger. "I said a lot of things on those nights. The last thing I said was that I can't do this anymore. I need you to listen to those words and nothing else. You have to go. And please, don't come here again. Promise me."

There was a protracted pause, and the package was dropped to the asphalt. It broke open, a swatch of white cloth landing on the grubby floor. "Watch this space, my love. I am your mage. This is the first of three gifts I have for you. When you receive the third, we'll talk again."

"Peter, I—"

Cutting her off, Peter waved his phone. "Before you go, can you take a look at this? You'll find it interesting, I promise. It's work related."

"I need to get back." Intrigue made her response lacklustre.

When he spoke, his voice had a teasing lilt. "It's a few seconds. Indulge me. You won't be sorry."

With a huff, she bent forwards to peer at the phone screen. In one smooth movement, Peter dropped his phone into his lap, scooped a hand around the nape of her neck, and dragged her towards him. His lips met hers, mashing them, his tongue licking her teeth, his free hand firm and rough upon her right breast.

She fought back, hard, her teeth biting his lower lip, making him cry out. She used the moment to pull herself away, her breathing ragged, the taste of his blood on her tongue.

"What the actual fuck?" she hissed. "Have you lost your mind?"

"Only when I'm around you, my love," he said, licking his bloodied lip. His eyes were alive and brimming with lust. "You're such an animal. I *want* you."

"Get out of here." Her tone was flat, dismissive. "Leave me alone."

His smile was serene. "Until next time, my love."

The window rose with a small hum, and the car pulled away, leaving Denise to track its journey until it disappeared behind a bend in the road.

She took a breath, heart pounding faster than it had ever been during her run. She headed home, *Fitbit* challenges muted by the bright swathes of guilt that come with infidelity.

Behind her, a brave rabbit watched from the hedgerow. Once she was a fair distance away, it checked out the road, making sure it was safe to cross. The creature moved with caution, stopping only to sniff at the discarded object lying in its path, and then it was on its way, leaving the box and its contents to the tyres of the pending traffic.

CHAPTER THREE

THE shower cubicle is gone, yet the space about him is no less confined: metal panels, a mirror, toilet of stainless steel, the blended and overpowering reek of piss and detergent. In his ears there is the reverberating roar of Rolls Royce engines. Beneath his feet the floor vibrates as the aircraft hits turbulence.

He can hear the 'ping-ping' of the seat belt signs going on. He looks to the mirror and sees a face that doesn't belong to him. It is bearded and the eyes are dark. A scar snakes down the left cheek. The man in the mirror is silently recounting the same phrase over and over.

His eyes drop down and the mirror is replaced by the sink unit. There is a grenade rattling around in the basin. It sends a metallic stutter through the cubicle until three heavy thuds on the toilet door have the man reaching for it. Ray can feel its weight as though the hands are his own.

"Sir? Are you okay?" The voice from behind the door is that of a woman with a Philly accent. When the man doesn't answer the voice returns. This time it has bite. "The light is on, sir. I need you to return to your seat."

Ray is no longer in the man, in the plane. He is soaring above the 737, looking down on it, watching the sun bouncing off the white fuselage in a series of bright starbursts. Then he hears the dull thud, sees the explosion near to the tail, a small thing that punches fire and flame and debris into the atmosphere where it is whipped away by the gale.

The 737's sleek outline buckles to a 'Z' shape. It reminds Ray of a bird riddled with buckshot falling from the sky. Then the plane breaks up into three pieces, disgorging its cargo as it tumbles through the clouds, the *howling wind indiscriminate in its assault, shredding paper, dismantling metal, bolt and pin, stripping bodies of their clothing.*

While his corporeal view affords much in terms of spectacle, his influence remains impotent. Yet this doesn't stop him screaming one word in a futile attempt to be heard above the wind.

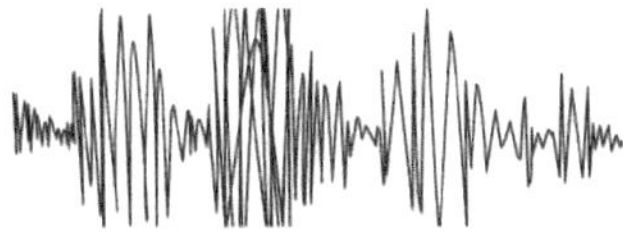

"No!"

Ray pressed his hands upon smooth, wet tile. If the hot water wasn't enough to rouse him, the post-vision headache was there to bring him into the here and now with the immediacy of fire alarm.

He fumbled for the shower controls, his head still bowed, hoping that the pounding jackhammer at his temples would take the edge off of his recollection of the 737's final moments. In days past, he would have fleetingly considered calling someone, demanding that something be done. Yet he knew that something *had* been done: a passenger plane, brought down by an act of terrorism—if not right now, then imminently. Such was the nature of his *abilities.*

Sluggishly, he climbed from the shower, towelling off before dressing for work. He picked up his ID badge, and read his role in life:

Ray Tonks: Clinical Risk Manager.

"Risk?"

The irony wasn't lost on him. He broke into laughter, gripping the nearby bath to take his weight, tears coursing down his face, the pain in his head threatening to pull his skull apart if he didn't stop. But he couldn't—wouldn't—for fear his mind made the decision to go for a morning stroll, and not come back.

He wiped his eyes on a towel and folded it, hanging it back on a towel rail coated in condensation. After several deep breaths, he opened the bathroom door and almost cried out in surprise when he saw Denise standing in the doorway.

"Shit. You scared me!"

Her smile was weary. "I'm not that hideous, am I?"

He thought he saw something else, a sparkle of sadness that came and went like a ghost. "Of course not. I'm not quite awake yet."

He gave her a peck on the cheek. She waved him off.

"Away with you, Mister. I need a shower." She looked into his eyes and a shadow crossed her face. "Have you been crying?"

"Um?"

"Your eyes are red. Have you been crying?"

"No, just got shower gel in them, that's all." It was a good lie, fast enough to get the job done.

"Oh." There it was—her interest gone. "Be a dear and put the kettle on. I'll be down in ten minutes."

The door closed and she was gone in a waft of perfumed sweat.

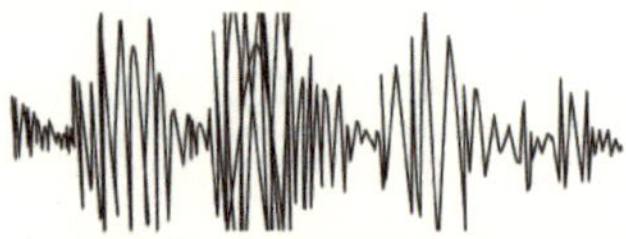

The digital radio on the windowsill was flanked by two Peace Lilies in black ceramic pots. In the time it took Denise to get ready for work, the news presenter had told Ray what he already knew. There were two huge news stories in one day. In Jakarta, the earthquake and subsequent tsunami had destroyed the city, and it was too early to determine the number of fatalities. The estimates from official sources were starting at 500,000, and were expected to climb as the authorities got boots on the chewed-up ground.

In another news item, a flight from Boston to Washington D.C. had been brought down, killing all on board, including the person who decided to grind a theological axe in a manner that only they could ever understand. The wreckage had been strewn over fifty square miles. One of the engines destroyed a farmer's grain silo in Delaware.

In a world beset by 'fake news', it was refreshing to have the assurance that anything coming out of presenter's mouth was actually true. Shame it took the deaths of so many to seal the deal.

Ray sat at the breakfast bar and sipped tea from a huge red mug with a Scooby-Doo motif on its surface. The mug represented him in many ways; it was old, yet still useful. Or at least he liked to think as much. This self-doubt was the product of having an ability that pretty much left him feeling the complete opposite. The news report, as they so often did, reinforced it to some degree. Time and again he thought about what the actual point was of having a sense that proved useless when it came to doing anything about preventing it. He sometimes felt that life was mocking him, and it often left him sullen and silent.

Just like his residual headaches, the dark moods were part and parcel of a post-vision. He tried to smooth them over, but being party to such trauma tended to put a stain on the day. There was always death and destruction, and always pain and despair. He'd considered whether, in another part of the world, there was someone who saw only positive things—the *Yin* to the *Yang*, so to speak—the universe making sure there was an ever-present state of equilibrium.

Such fanciful notions were never there for long. His visions were what they were and lies and deceit were now equally as much a part of him. Denise tolerated his 'illness' because he'd given it some semblance of credibility by grounding it with a medical label. But he sometimes felt his ruse was transparent to her; deceit pressing against the surface of his facade like an enduring, calculating predator waiting to break through and claim all he held dear.

But this wasn't just down to the lies or the pressures of someone living with neurodivergence. Their marriage had weathered storms and found tranquil waters long ago, but now it languished in a sea of apathy, a Sargasso Sea, always under the threat of sliding off the map to a place marked 'Here There Be Monsters'. A place where Ray didn't wish to dwell, in fear he'd uncover the kind of abominations that spouted home truths instead of fire and teeth.

There was still love, that's the way he saw it. But you'd have to look for it beneath the familiarity.

And Denise?

Well, he hadn't asked her in quite a while, afraid that her 'I love you' and bi-monthly cavort under the covers were nothing more than token platitudes; day to day duties no different to filling the dishwasher or taking out the garbage.

They'd talked of kids, tried for them even. But for some reason it didn't happen. Biological incompatibility saw to that, their careers did the rest. And time? Well, it worked its magic and created a languid world where one day became no different to another. It shouldn't have worked, but it did, the stability creating a safe haven from the powerful interludes the visions brought to him.

"Are you working late today?" Denise asked, taking a carton of milk to her cereal.

"Yes. Finalising papers for the damn Governance Committee. Why?"

"Thought I'd go and catch a movie."

"Anything we could go see together?"

"Not really. It's a chick flick. Thought I'd go with Amy. You know, from work?"

He used tea to swallow his disappointment. "Okay."

Something buzzed in his ears—a distortion—and for a moment he thought the digital radio had suddenly lost a channel. Denise's words became static fizz, and he looked up at her, his own mouth open, but his query never left his lips.

Oblivious, his wife opened the milk carton and poured a thin stream into the cereal bowl. Ray watched the milky cataract, drawn to it, fascinated by it, the *flow* of it. No, that wasn't quite right. It didn't quite *flow*, did it? It *oozed*. And it wasn't ivory anymore, not really. It was pink—like a strawberry shake—the simile made even more effective by the sickly stink of ripe berries that came with it. With each passing moment the pink milk was turning to red—bright red—as though it was blood.

He sucked in air as he looked at his wife.

The thing sitting across the table may well have had Denise's body, but the face was a frozen mask of gold and blue, lips fixed in a pout. The eye-sockets were feline, but there were no iris or corneas—only a grey, vacillating mass of pixels.

Blood began to pour from the mouth, the lips still pursed as a thin line appeared across the delicate, white throat and the head slipped forwards, leaving only a stump of a neck behind.

In a quasi-dreamlike state, the head landed on the table, upending the cereal bowl, then rolled, coming to stop on its left cheek, hair matted with milk and gore, the bowl trapped beneath it like some comical, ceramic hat.

And to his horror, Ray heard a gurgling, hissing voice that was distorted by blood and severed vocal cords.

"I'm so empty."

Ray pushed his body away from the table and emptied his guts onto the linoleum, his hands clutching his knees, his shoes and socks slick with his breakfast.

With resolve, he pulled his eyes back to the table where Denise stared back at him. She was talking again, though this time her head was where it was supposed to be.

Her voice was firm, yet edged with disgust. "And you can clear *that* up before you go to work."

CHAPTER FOUR

RAY drove his Audi Q4 to the local train station. After parking up, he headed inside a building made up of red brick and shimmering glass facias before navigating flights of stairs and concourses to get to the platform. The station was abuzz with other commuters, giving him the hint that there were going to be very few seats up for grabs, something they never seemed to feature in the railway advertising, nor acknowledged in the escalating ticket price.

An announcement boomed from the overhead speakers, the bright and optimistic tone telling everyone the train was running ten minutes late. The grumbled response from the platform made it clear not everyone was as accepting of the news.

Ray waited, the crackle of the sound system forcing his mind back to the most recent vision as he tried to decipher its meaning. His revulsion over the images he'd witnessed at breakfast hadn't dimmed with time, not merely because of the horror of it, but because it had *felt* different.

First of all, there had been no pain. Not before, not during, and no residual headache in the aftermath. Then, there was the manner in which the vision rolled. The thing on the table had spoken to him. Interaction wasn't a usual part of the deal. Ray had never known a time where he'd been anything more than an onlooker to the terrible events as they unfolded within his mind's eye, a mere fly on the wall in the world's biggest shitshow. He tried to garner some of the optimism present in the recent disembodied voice that had told everyone their train was delayed. He thought that, maybe, this change in presentation meant that he could do something before such tragedies happened. *If* he could understand what the fuck it all meant, of course. In truth, he knew nothing about his ability; he had no real context or grounding to draw upon.

He looked up as if hoping to find answers, but found only a flock of geese cruising in a 'V' at high altitude. He wondered where they were heading, not surprised to find that his next thought asked the same question of him.

The sudden, general shift in the crowd indicated the train was in sight, and sure enough, the amiable voice on the Tannoy system confirmed its arrival. As the engine pulled into the station, Ray moved with the crowd, a lemming swept towards the edge of the platform. The train stopped, the access doors passing him by several feet. Any chance of a seat disappeared as the other commuters climbed aboard, leaving him and other less fortunate passengers to board and stand in the aisles.

As the train lurched on its way, he clutched at the handrail, his palms slick against the plastic. The carriage shimmied in a steady rhythm as the train progressed towards the city, where his workplace of twenty years waited for him.

His role as a clinical risk manager was worlds apart from where he started out. Back in the mid-eighties, he'd made the decision to embark on a career in mental health nursing; an offshoot from the daily challenges of having a mother with clinical depression. These days, he was riled by the notion that depression was the go-to diagnosis whenever people felt fed-up or thwarted by the realities of life. He was frustrated by some people's apparent obsession to collect more labels than those stuck to Paddington Bear's iconic suitcase. The internet didn't help, of course. Social media was fast becoming a theatre full of bad actors. He felt that all of this cheapened the actuality of living with mental illness, a life where any sense of hope was under constant threat, risking a perpetual darkness that sucked the desire to live from every waking moment. His mother succumbed to the call in the summer of 1983. She'd got up one morning while he was at college and went for a stroll to a northbound flyover on the M5 motorway, where she jumped and found oblivion beneath an eighteen-wheeler heading to Sheffield.

His grief was tempered by the thought that somewhere beneath all of the tragedy, there was mercy in the outcome. Yes, he felt guilty at drawing such a conclusion, but ultimately, it galvanised feelings that he could help those who seemed helpless at an earlier stage of the illness.

So, he went to a school of nursing and undertook the three year programme to become a Registered Mental Nurse (or RMN) and staffed in many services: acute admissions, forensics, working with older people and, finally, in speciality services such as the Deaf Community, and those with a diagnosis of Borderline Personality Disorder. During this time, he'd seen the literal highs and lows of mental illness, worked with people in the spirit of recovery—giving hope in a potentially hopeless world—and had to manage the associated risks that came with such interventions.

Risks were tangible in Ray's game. They encompassed those of the person, the environment, and the risk to others. Over time, he realised it was the latter that often made the news. A headline splashed across tabloids—ill-informed, yet the outcome was provocative enough; the irrepressible work of charities like *MIND* or *Rethink* to challenge stigma, undone when those tortured by their illness harmed a member of the public. Ray understood the response, of course. Anyone hurt (or worse, killed) could only be seen as a tragedy, yet he was able to navigate press bias—look beyond the inflammatory words of contempt and ignorance—and see *everyone* as a victim. This was forever a trait he was happy to embrace.

He'd migrated from staff nurse to ward manager, and then went on to become a matron, where his role focused on clinical risk, its management, and the quality associated with it. He headed investigations, interviewed staff, service users, their families and their carers, generating reports in order to learn lessons, to improve things, and thus create clinical climates to keep everyone safe. He was meticulous and fastidious, and very good at it. It was only a matter of time before he moved away from actual clinical services and into the Risk Management Department, where his skills and knowledge could be utilised at a strategic level. It was in his role as Clinical Risk Manager where he'd excelled and remained for the past decade.

In the carriage, someone jostled him, bringing him back to the present. He let it pass—bumping into people was an occupational hazard when commuting on a shitty rail service. Everyone in the same proverbial boat, even if that boat had *Titanic* stencilled on the hull. Still, he looked up from his reverie.

And found himself gawping into the face that defied logic.

Yet it was a face that was all too familiar, because he had seen it that morning before it had landed on the breakfast bar. The same mask-like face, the eyes still a grey, flickering mess like that of a TV screen caught between channels. He blinked twice, his brain struggling to register the incongruity the image brought. The figure had a woman's body, a long black coat, a white blouse, a skirt that stopped off at pink knees.

He whispered, aghast. "What are you? What are you doing here?"

"I feel so empty," the indefinable face said. Like the response, the voice was vague and distant, a parody as devoid of congruity as the oscillating face it came from. Its tone was discordant, as though several people were saying the same words all at once.

There was something behind the woman with the frozen face, a creeping shadow. It rose like a black sun from over her left shoulder, the head a collage of silver stitches, the eyes and mouth zippered slits. This contorted effigy writhed backwards and forwards like a cobra ready to strike, and in its ebony, stitched hands, it held a vial of red liquid.

Ray opened his mouth to speak, but his lips froze as he noticed a pool of claret spreading across the woman's abdomen as though she'd spilt a glass of Shiraz on her top. The ghastly shadow had upended the vial and was pouring its contents onto the material of the woman's blouse, the stain blossoming, the material distending as though something of substance was pushing against it, forcing the buttons apart, the gaps between them revealing glistening fat tubes, grey and slick with gore.

He took a step backwards, letting go of the handrail, the floor beneath him juddering as the train took a bend. He lost his balance and bumped into the person next to him—a rotund man in a pin-striped suit.

"Careful, you idiot," the man snapped, but the voice seemed as though it was coming to Ray through water. He squeezed his eyes closed, a child trying to shut out the reproach of a parent. In this act, he heard a heavy slap as if something large and wet had hit the floor.

He opened his eyes, afraid of what vile image would be waiting for him, but found only the searing stares of the other passengers.

"Sorry," he said to the disapproving faces about him. Mercifully, neither the shadow-creature nor the gutted woman was among them. "I lost my footing."

"You need to watch what you're having for breakfast," a woman in a white blouse and raincoat said.

Ray gave her a small smile, trying his best not to look down at her blouse, just in case it began seeping blood.

CHAPTER FIVE

The first thing Ray did when he got off the train was send a text message to Denise. It was a simple edict; three words that he hoped would give him peace of mind.

Are you okay?

He walked along the platform and was approaching the stairway leading up to the exit barriers when the phone buzzed in his hand. He looked down at the screen, the disorientation blurring his vision as his eyes made their adjustments.

Yes.

He nodded and paused, ignoring the mutterings from people who'd had to navigate around him to get to the stairway. Family was always more important, especially during times of crisis.

The act of getting in touch with Denise was instinctual and based on events that had happened over breakfast. Yet there had been no indication in his vision that his wife was in any danger. Still, he couldn't shake the gnawing feeling that these latest experiences were somehow different than usual. The fact that he could put some kind of normalcy tag to his abilities was in itself surprising, but in the end, he figured that acceptance was the only way to live with such an incredible mandate on a day to day basis.

Every little thing helps, he thought as he exited the station and stepped outside, onto the plaza.

He suppressed a chuckle, but with his astonishment, it continued regardless, building into a guffaw as he found that he no longer had control over his vocal cords. Oblivious, the people around him continued about their business, and Ray realised that he was having some kind of dissociative episode.

He continued to laugh, but inside, felt only the pervading terror of losing his mind. There was something else—a giggle—crawling beneath his laughter, usurping the din, slithering into his brain, making itself at home, the way maggots writhe and burrow into spoiled meat.

The sound that came from his mouth did not belong to him. It was malevolent and deep, bubbling like a throat choked up with phlegm. In confusion, he turned to face the station doors and reeled as he caught sight of his reflection in the glass panels. His body was now a writhing mass; a nebulous, pulsating cloud that broiled on the air. He tried to scream, but all that came was the utterance of some-one—*something*—else.

"The darkness yearns like a lover. Embrace it."

About him, the station and the plaza began to sink as a river of *nothingness* broke its banks, inky black waters pouring into streets, consuming all. This belligerent tide brought with it waves of despair and fear and anger and hate, irrational, irrepressible, the force of it making Ray scream as though succumbing to madness. The voice came again, this time in his ear, whispering, so close he could feel the heat of its foul breath.

"Come. Accept what has been given."

"No, no, for the love of God, NO!"

The vision ended abruptly, an unkept man in a furrowed tracksuit staring into his face.

"What the fuck is wrong with you?"

Ray blinked away the nightmare, his brain still muddied by its touch.

"You on something?" the guy sounded hopeful, his heavy eyebrows arched with expectation. "You *got* any?"

"No," Ray said shaking his head clear. "I have to go. Thank you for your concern."

But the man grabbed hold of Ray's arm, preventing him from walking away. "I want whatever you've got," he said, his tone firm. "And I want it *now!*"

"Take your hand off me."

As Ray said the words, he felt something shift in his mind, as if the thought had followed his words out into the world. To his amazement, the man's face went slack, his eyes blank, and his hand fell away from Ray's arm.

Ray hurried off, not looking back until he was at the other side of the plaza, by which time his would-be mugger was gone.

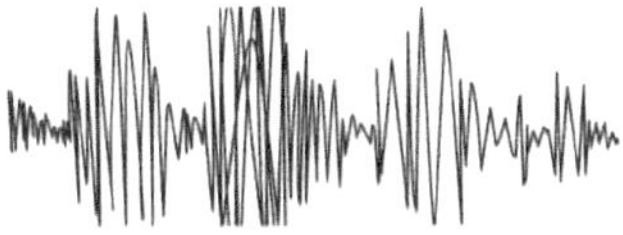

The Trust Headquarters was on the outskirts of the city, a logistical far cry from the wards and units under its jurisdiction. There were three hospital sites, sixty different wards, and five different services, the governance of which came from the offices of Davenport House, a Victorian building of red brick that had been restored to its former glories back in the mid-eighties, when the HQ had uprooted and found new lodgings in a far more accessible area of the city.

Like many office workers, Ray's desk was an extension of his personality— individuality amid the uniform. As such, his workstation was the epitome of tidiness, a tranquil isle in the mezzanine maelstrom around him.

There was a silver, triple-frame photograph, embossed with a swan motif, wings spread in two-dimensional flight. At one point in time, it had been on a fire surround in their second home together. Now it took pride of place, flanked by a paperweight—a conch trapped in glass from a day trip to Weston-Super-Mare—and a heavy duty stapling machine.

The photograph in the centre was taken when Denise had been celebrating getting her MSc in Health Studies from the University of Birmingham. She wore a cap and gown, paired with a proud smile. Ray remembered a time when the picture had been in a white frame and hung in a downstairs toilet in their first home. He'd never understand why a loo wall was a fitting place to display such achievement. It seemed an act of embarrassment, although he knew that Denise was far from bashful when it came to her professional achievements. He'd always meant to ask her why she'd chosen to display the photo in such an inauspicious place, but like so many things lost to a busy life, such inclination only seemed to come to mind when at his work desk.

The frame to the left was a picture with them both sitting at the base of a crossroads sign at Land's End, Cornwall. They'd been on their honeymoon, and Ray had asked a fellow tourist to take it with an old, beaten up Nikon A7. The autofocus was off and the image was slightly blurred. Denise used to laugh and say it was a portent to whatever mysteries life had in store for them. Ray had laughed too, somehow managing to supress the inherent unease that came whenever he heard reference to *portentous* moments.

As well as his family keepsakes, the computer monitor had a Windows pre-loaded screensaver, some image of a mountain range that no one but photographers with a travel budget get to see. In the cobalt sky above this precipitous, onscreen landscape, four folders hovered—indexed and tiered in alphabetical order.

Sometimes he found this place a sanctuary from the unpredictability of his blackouts; a safe haven, order captured in the workspace. It made him feel calm whenever he laid his eyes upon it.

Given the intense and confounding nature of the psychological upheaval he'd endured so far that morning, he'd take solace from wherever he could get it.

On the desk next to Ray, a VDU rose from a cluttered, disorderly landscape made from piles of paper and thick, green files. A large red coffee mug with the slogan 'SEVEN DAY WEEKEND' was standing proud next to a Polar Gear lunchbox. A discarded chocolate bar wrapper and empty 'Bombay Bad Boy' Pot Noodle carton completed this physical manifestation of sloth. For those who didn't get the hint from the state of the desk, the presence of the large man sitting at it would have consolidated the deal.

Mike Tanner had a wiry beard and steel framed glasses. His eyes were as blue as the shapeless shirts he usually wore. His outlook on life was often as dark as his trousers and heavy boots, and he always carried with him the slight odour of hamster cages.

As the team's data analyst, what Mike lacked in people skills he made up for in focus and objective reasoning. This was a good thing in that it made him exceptional at his job, and this was why Ray was far more tolerant of the slovenly attitude than others.

"Shit, boss," Mike said as Ray approached his desk. "You look like you only just left the party."

Ray tutted. "Mike, we talked about this. You've got to watch your language at work."

Mike's reply was genuinely contrite. "Fuck, yeah—oops—sorry. I forgot."

Shaking his head, Ray went over to his workstation. About him, the mezzanine stretched out for over a hundred metres square, many desks, photocopy machines and filing cabinets dotted here and there, and at the far end of the floor, a row of rooms waited for the first meetings of the day.

Ray sat down, pushing back in his chair. His mind was trying to focus on his computer and erase the troublesome thoughts cluttering his brain.

He sensed someone standing beside him and looked up, eyes squinting.

"You want some paracetamol, Ray?"

Eloise Adebola's concerned expression put creases into her otherwise unblemished forehead. Her dark eyes scanned Ray's face. She was young, and pretty, and an incredibly talented risk assessor. In her navy blue trouser suit she exuded professionalism, the antithesis of Mike's languor.

Ray pinched the bridge of his nose and squeezed his eyes closed. "No, I'm good, thanks. Just give me a minute, it'll pass."

He sucked in air, held onto it until his lungs ached, then let it out. The discomfort faded to a dull pulse in his temple. He thought he'd got away with the headache. Trust him to jump to conclusions. Part of it was hoping that there were no residual effects this time. On occasions, the headaches would leave him bed bound, chewing on Tylenol for six hours. This time round, it seemed as though he was going to get cut some slack. *Thank the heavens for small mercies*, his mother had often said. The irony of her adage wasn't lost on him.

"Better?" Eloise asked.

Ray opened his eyes, his peripheral vision shimmering for a few seconds as he blinked the prism away.

It did not return.

After a few moments, he nodded to Eloise and Mike. "Good enough. Thanks for the support, guys. Lunch is on me today."

Mike gave a mock salute. "Fuckin' 'A', boss."

Ray stared at the analyst.

Mike grinned. "Is this where you give me another bollocking?"

Relishing the reprieve, Ray returned his smile.

CHAPTER SIX

THE tabloid press calls you 'Frankenstein'. While this is quaint, you are far from a work of fiction. You are as true as the sun is a star, and in moments such as these, you share its splendour amid the heavens.

Right now, your breathing is smooth, despite the effort it has taken to bring to fruition the scene laid out before you. The cupboards and surfaces are featureless—clinical—a place of chrome and steel, brought to life by the fluorescents. While you are prepared to do your work here, this is <u>not</u> your place of work. Like many things in your life, the space has been borrowed, temporarily absorbed into your existence the way a mountain swallows a serpentine road, so it may continue to other places. Such preparation takes guile—a nuance of sorts—as your latest project lies inert on the shimmering table, a monument to incalculable patience.

The killing isn't what drives you; it is a means to an end. What motivates is connection, the need to be part of something, feeling whole in a severed, separate world. You know how you got here—you have insight after all—and it is perhaps because of this that you are able to garner the deep seated love associated with your actions, and what others would see as the incomprehensible horror of butchering another human being.

To those versed in human anatomy—forensic pathologists, for instance—your actions make more sense, even if the psychology behind them does not. And how could they know without sitting down and digging deep, the way you sometimes delve into both body cavity and skull in the search of a greater truth? They do not know this yearning to be complete that drives you, how the mere act of cohesion satisfies something so profound within you, it leaves you weeping as you give thanks.

Such feelings are addictive, of course. That is why you must continue *with purpose, and ignore the trivial day-to-day distractions provided by a chameleon lifestyle, built over many years. You have been loved, you relish the touch of another, and you have indeed reciprocated in kind.*

But it is in the here and now you must focus, the body on the table is waiting for you, waiting for your love. And, in turn, it will fulfil you; meeting the basic needs that snarl like angry, cornered dogs, held at bay only by the commands of their master. Because, despite what the world may think, there is love in your actions—in the planning, the execution, in the ending of a life.

But true love comes when you take your scalpel to the body, slicing and opening the flesh.

And sigh in contentment as your subject finally gives up its gifts.

CHAPTER SEVEN

MIKE had decided he didn't like people at a relatively early age. Over time, he had concluded that the human race, more often than not, sucked like a horny 'Hetty' vacuum cleaner.

The breeding ground that was to help him shape such an abject conclusion was his experience of school. He was, by nature, a shy soul, and drawn to solitary pursuits, finding the concept of sports—competition in any guise, for that matter—completely abhorrent.

An only child, he was raised by parents who were quiet and sensitive, and destined to have a son imbued with such traits. Family holidays were sedate affairs, cultured trips to museums and galleries around the world, nurturing his love for the arts and his endless desire to be creative. This showed him there was a side to humanity that was not seduced by an innate directive for destruction.

This edict was tested through the years. His own experience of how kids saw people who were different did not leave him with such optimism. His so-called 'schoolmates' were, in fact, a bunch of lower-middle-class kids, born to parents who thought that they were more than they actually were: middle-managers, owners of small businesses, wannabe entrepreneurs who, in reality, equated to bad conmen with drive.

None of this was to matter to a young Mike, who was the brunt of abuse and bullying, the school considering it no more than 'boisterous behaviour' rather than admit they had an endemic problem that they were ultimately letting get out of control. This wasn't helped, of course, by the main ringleader being intrinsic to the school football team, and their parent's tenure on the Board of

Governors.

Bullshit, all of it.

Such events were to shape his attitudes over time, and no one would have blamed him. He rebelled against his parents, who, at that point, he felt were ineffective; their approach of rationale argument proving pretty much futile despite their tenacity with the Headteacher. Complaints to OFSTED followed, but without evidence, it was discounted. His parents saw their son's frustration, felt him try to disconnect at their perceived inaction, so they did what they could to keep him safe, choosing instead to homeschool him.

That was how it went until he successfully passed his GCSEs and went to the local college to do A-Levels, and during his time in educational exile, Mike had grown physically—he was standing well over six-six, and his staple diet of junk food and zero exercise had taken its toll. He was a mountain of a youth, yet he was far, far happier.

At college, he met several like-minded souls, and still kept contact with these friends, even when he went to university to study for a BSc in Computer Science. Being young and impressionable, social skills were borrowed from his peers, and on occasion, he had problems adapting to social convention, his inappropriate use of choice language being a case in point.

Expecting his boss to be on his back pretty much all of the time, Mike was surprised when Ray was genuinely interested in his worldview. And what was more impressive was that Mike felt as though his boss actually tried to *understand* it. In this, Mike found he had deep respect for Ray. Slowly, his mistrust drifted away to the periphery of his life at work, but it never disappeared completely.

This became all too obvious when Eloise came to join their department and, for Mike's emotional stability, waged a quiet war.

She'd arrived to work with the team a few years ago after their last risk assessor (a quiet and wholesome woman by the name of Janet, who had reminded Mike of his own mother) had retired early to look after her sick husband. Mike had figured that Ray, by way of a replacement, wanted someone who was experienced and dynamic, elements that would give the department some longevity. Even with his naturally suspicious nature, Mike could recognise the logic of such a mandate. But he found Eloise *very* attractive, and quite a distraction from the mundane existence to which he'd become accustomed.

If his experiences at school had left him somewhat socially awkward, then his ability to comfortably interact with someone like Eloise was beyond definition. In the first few weeks, he'd not been able to string a cohesive sentence together, finding that his face burned as though exposed to the hottest sun whilst wearing the shittiest sunscreen.

He could see that, despite being incredibly beautiful, she was also patient, and this helped him adapt in the coming months. When he thought about these things now, he couldn't believe he'd been such a dickhead in those early days.

Again, it was Ray who had smoothed the discord. A team meeting where everyone spoke a little about themselves—disclosure in a bid to bevel the edges_made their team fit together. Within three months, Mike could not remember a time Eloise had never worked there, and her earnest gratitude for his efficiency helping to cement their working relationship.

Professional respect is what made their affiliation work, and in the back of his mind, way back behind the barriers of low self-esteem, part of him wished they could have been closer—more than just colleagues. Whenever such a notion came to him, he would smother it in self-deprecating laughter and move his mind on to more realistic occurrences.

He always had his hobby to turn to, after all.

When emotions became too intense, Mike would always default to his *hobby*. He enjoyed making things. Creating a beautiful whole from so many different parts was an act of both science and art. Above all, it gave him a sense of peace that he could never find in people.

But his hobby wasn't something he could shout about. People would not understand, and there was a danger that they would react negatively to how he spent his time alone. The hobby had been born from trauma and guilt, bad times in those early days of chaos and rebellion. When he thought about such origins—the terrible emotional pain it had taken to gestate his gift—Mike would stall and abandon his work for a few months. The desire always came back because his hobby was now a significant part of who he was—it just had to be covert.

His *little secret*.

No matter how quiet the moment, some things were never meant to be spoken aloud.

CHAPTER EIGHT

ELOISE sat hunched over her keypad, her fingers deftly moving across the keys in a steady stream, filling her workspace with tiny, staccato clicks. On the screen, another sentence crossed the document, the report almost finished, another deadline smashed.

She prided herself on being efficient; it was a trait that made her feel content and useful. Such things were never far away from her, because Eloise's life could have been—*should* have been—very different.

At four years of age she had been put into care by her mother, a heroin user who, in one final moment of clarity, had handed her daughter over to the authorities, unable to cope. Three months later her birthmother would be dead, and her father—of whom Eloise had no memory—was nowhere to be found. Foster care came next, several families who found that a young Eloise had exacted her sense of loss on their homes—smashing up her bedroom, and, in one instance, throwing a kitchen knife at a foster carer. The sense of loss, the desperation to adjust, brought to bear on those who tried to care for her.

By the time she was six, she'd met Mark and Tiffany Stephenson, a middle-aged couple with significant experience in managing challenging behaviours in kids. Mark was a retired child and adolescent mental health worker. Special Officer status meant that he had retired on a full NHS pension at fifty-five years of age. Tiffany was a nursery nurse, ten years his junior, but whether it was their calm and warm demeanour or their experience of working with vulnerable children, Eloise connected with the couple, at that time not even registering that Mark was a black African and his wife an Irish redhead with an effervescent personality.

Laughter was ever present in the Stephenson household, and was welcomed by a young girl for which mirth and merriment had been absent for most of her life. Within two years of being with Mark and Tiffany, Eloise had been asked if she would like for them to adopt her and raise her as their own daughter. When she said yes, they had all sat on a big leather sofa and cried, then followed that up with an afternoon of ice cream and Disney movies.

Her relationship with Mark was to become a close one, bridging the gap left by her absent, biological father. As time went on, this relationship made her feel complete in ways she simply could never explain.

During the next ten years, Eloise's behaviours stabilised, the affection and warmth shown to her by the Stephenson household getting her life back on track. Her school teachers found that she had a gift for abstract thinking, yet also an aptitude for organisation. It wasn't unusual for her parents to see *High School Musical* calendars filled with important dates, usually things such as school trips and birthdays, but as time went on, the side of the fridge in the kitchen found itself a home for exam and revision timetables, and an ever-growing collection of school achievement certificates, all secured with fridge magnets. Eloise always had an interest in how the human body worked, and excelled in the sciences, especially biology and chemistry.

Good high school grades took her to college, where she aced her A-Levels with three A*s and went to Exeter to study biology. Life, it seemed, was giving her rewards for those tumultuous early years, but in the first year at university, Eloise found out that there was to be payback when her father was killed in the street.

The reports suggested that he tried to break up a fight between two youths, a knife was pulled, and he got in the way. He died two weeks later in the ICU, and Tiffany derailed soon after, depression becoming a blueprint for the year ahead. The kid went down for manslaughter, but the Stephenson family paid the greater price.

It was at this time that Eloise struggled with her own demons. The four-year-old child who had lost everything resurfaced for a time. It was brief yet intense, and to some degree left her off-kilter ever since. In those few months, she learned that a past can never truly be forgotten, nor could it fail to have some influence over the future. Following her father's funeral—an event of such emotional intensity she often still dreamed of it—she wrestled with psychological conflicts, and found solace of sorts in accepting very quickly who she was and the means by which she kept herself whole. From that point forward, her ability to detach herself from the trauma, almost with clinical efficiency, would prove to be a boon in all her life choices, but the interim focus had been pretty clear in those days following her father's death.

She put her studies on hold, initially for a year as she nursed her mother, then indefinitely as Tiffany emerged from her fugue as a fragile entity, prone to melancholy and a displaced demeanour.

At one point, alcohol was prominent, but it was Eloise's presence that prevented dependency from taking hold. It was to be four more years before time (and medication) had healed the psychological wounds. By then, Eloise was working in the local supermarket as a floor supervisor, and living with her mother in a home now mortgage free due to the terrible fate of her father.

It was Tiffany who suggested that she should reapply to university. They had been sitting in the lounge, a place of so much laughter in the past. Now the atmosphere was still, with only the ticking of the clock on the mantelpiece filling in the blanks.

"You have to start looking out for yourself, Ellie," her mother had said.

"And who is going to look out for *you*?"

Tiffany had responded with a tired smile. "Well, I guess it's about time I took back the reins. You need to get yourself a good job."

"I've *got* a good job. Plus, it's nearby. I'm not seeing any downsides."

"Then you're looking in the wrong places, honey," Tiffany had replied, sadly. "You've spent so much of your time babysitting your old mum, you've yet to live."

Eloise had thought this over. Then she'd shaken her head. "I have all I need right here."

"You were never meant to work in any shop, good or bad. And you need to be enjoying life. Get yourself someone to settle down with."

"Are you writing me off already?"

"You *know* what I mean. I have money left from your father's life insurance. We can get you back to university. Go and finish that course you started. You deserve that, at least." Tiffany's eyes were bright with enthusiasm, and it had been such a long time since Eloise had seen such a thing, she relented after the briefest of pauses.

"Okay, you win," she'd said, hugging her mother. "But I have conditions. First, I pay my way. I have savings to contribute, and I won't take 'no' for an answer. And second, I'm going to the local university, and staying here, *at home*. If you agree to that, then I'll put in an application for next year. Deal?"

Her mother had agreed, and that was the way it went for the next four years, Eloise returning to university via an 'access to learning' course she'd undertaken through an online distance education platform. There, she found her mind returning to her natural aptitude for learning and abstract thought. This time, however, she had some steer. The time spent looking after her mother had shaped her in more ways than she truly understood. She found her work leaning towards risk and healthcare, finally concluding the degree with a piece of research on mental illness and clinical risk, earning her a First on results day.

She was encouraged by her tutor (a seasoned and passionate lady named Paulette Fuller) to apply for a master's degree and, with her mother's backing, studied Risk Management and Healthcare before coming out of university with a glowing resume and two degrees.

Paulette sought out her contacts in the local Mental Healthcare Trust, using the staunch connections between academic and healthcare organisations. She recommended Eloise to a good friend in the risk management department, securing her an interview when a post came up.

That was over three years ago, and in that time, Eloise had revelled in the challenges of her role—excelled in it, point of fact. Promotions came fast, and her ability to adapt thrived in the ever-changing world of NHS healthcare.

She had her pastimes: the gym, and her friends. She had plenty of time to kill since her mother passed away. It had been two years since the cancer settled in and staked its claim. Tiffany had been diagnosed in the spring and was dead by the summer. Eloise had been with her at the end, and the final moments were nothing but a relief to both of them. She had watched a woman of great substance visibly shrink. In the final days of her life, Tiffany's usually amiable face had been pulled into nothing more than a mask of pain. Morphine had been ramped up and did its job on a desperately frail respiratory system.

The funeral was a sedate affair, with just a few scattered relatives huddled together around the grave. Eloise watched her mother's coffin descend, and that clinical detachment threatened to yank her away from the event. This desire to disconnect was a defence mechanism—a throwback to her early years, she knew this now. It had never been as intense as it was at her parent's funerals, but she stood her ground and took it on. Her father's death had set the groundwork, her mother's funeral was where it came to fruition. She'd fought against it, inwardly cursing its presence. She was *meant* to feel this; she'd *needed* to feel it, to be connected with the last person in her life who really meant something to her.

The phone to her right rang out and she quietly thanked its intrusion. There were plenty of other times to rake over such things.

She answered the phone and, as always, used work to cast out her demons.

CHAPTER NINE

TRUE to his word, Ray did indeed pay for lunch. The trio trooped out of the building and walked to a pelican crossing that spanned two lanes of heavy traffic. The air tasted of diesel, and the tendrils of heavy smoke from articulated waggons looked like spectres hitching a lift.

Their destination was a small café several hundred yards from their offices. It was a sedate place, gaining just enough trade to turn a comfortable profit while still keeping a small, and loyal, clientele.

As they traversed the road, Eloise chatted amicably about work matters. Mike had his hands dug deeply into his heavy Donkey Jacket, headphones in situ as he mouthed the words of the unheard tune.

Ray's attention flitted from the conversations between his work colleagues to the busy street, all the time trying to push away errant thoughts of his recent visions and the sudden change in how they were presenting.

He could not, and would not, ever consider his visions to be 'normal', but they were as much a part of him as his heart and soul. As he considered the shifting nuances of recent events, much to his chagrin, his mind travelled back to the time when all of this shit first began.

The images of a schoolyard took a stroll through his mind. He saw other kids charging around, blue and gold ties, black blazers and trousers, uniformed tearaways hell-bent on making sure their shoes never lasted any longer than a term. He'd been equally as boisterous—equally as to blame—for what happened on that afternoon recess, where sense and stupidity blurred in one instant to create a lifetime of skewed misery.

It began when an eight-year-old Wayne Phillips—a school friend that Ray would eventually lose touch with when they both went to university—forgot to bring his tennis ball to school. The ball was their solace in that space between lessons, and the six-a-side football game was their sanctuary from the pent-up frustrations of being cooped up in a classroom on a 1970s summer day. Without the ball, tensions boiled over with grumbling and muttering that left Wayne desperately trying to find an alternative. The games of 'tag' and 'tick-on-release' were discounted as being 'too girly'. The memory had Ray allowing the corners of his mouth to curve upwards slightly.

These days, such labels would be grounds for a person being cancelled in the frenzied cyber-world of social media. How times had changed. Morality and tolerance were always uneasy bedfellows, with the threat of divorce never too far away. For good or ill, he had no view on such mandates, other than that life was for living, and a person needed to do what they could to glean whatever happiness that was on offer.

Like telling your wife a few lies about neurological issues, just to keep things ticking over. Or, back in that 1970s school yard, making a madcap suggestion that, with hindsight, was as reckless as it was life changing.

In the school yard, the suggestion that was to change Ray's life forever came quickly. Wayne went over to the edge of the playground, where a mesh fence was lashed to concrete posts, and at the base, began scrabbling around in the dirt. Ray and the others had watched him, catcalls and sniggering becoming a soundtrack to his bizarre behaviour.

Wayne returned with a hefty, dirt clotted pebble, left behind when the fence had been erected. Dropping the stone to the ground, Wayne had kicked it around a few times to dislodge the dry earth. Ray and those around him started to laugh, but this petered out as the desire to rescue their game took over. In a second, it was decided that their tournament would continue using the pebble. And for the first ten minutes, everything went remarkably well.

And then came 'the incident'.

Ray had been told about what had happened afterwards by Wayne, and the term 'incident' had been used a lot in the investigation that followed. The last thing that Ray could recall was the pebble coming off the foot of a boy by the name of Gaz Adams, the shoe digging deep, sending their makeshift football into the air, and the total and utter moment of complete madness where instinct took precedent, and Ray went up to meet it, the intention to head it into the goal. He recalled the mouths of those around him opening to shout out what he now knew to be a warning. His head connected with the pebble over his right eye, and then blackness took him.

He'd woken up three days later, the faces of his worried parents looming over him, the relief captured in their eyes, on his mother's lips as she kissed him over and over almost overpowering him.

The doctors said he'd sustained a hairline fracture to his skull but felt the prognosis was very good, as long as he didn't try to headbutt any more rocks. His father had grumbled something about the event maybe knocking some sense into his foolhardy son, and they had all laughed—the relief palpable to all.

Yet the relief was to be short-lived. Aa few days later, Ray had experienced his first vision.

At first, the images had come as mere flashes, like ghostly shapes in a room lit by lightning. A boy holding hands with a tall man the day before little Timmy Weston was taken and found in a brook one week later, dead and defiled.

The terrible image of old man Clutterbuck, his body bent and broken as the Ford Transit hit him on the pelican crossing, spinning him five times before his already shattered remains buckled on impact against the asphalt.

No matter how or when the visions came, they were to become as much a part of his life as his regret of ever trying to head that fucking pebble.

Closing off these niggling thoughts, he focused on going to get lunch, his colleagues blissfully unaware of his trials.

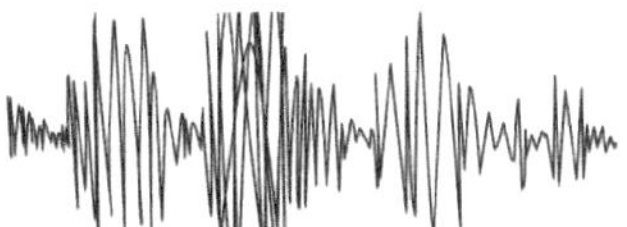

Smooth and firm, yet oh, so delicate, this precious thing held in coveted hands, hands that will unite the disparate; so many pieces that will make one, remarkable whole.

This is a special place, an altar of sorts, where creation is revered. Needle and thread are the means by which perfection comes to life. The fingers holding these elements are seasoned and expert. There is no hesitancy, no hint of doubt as they execute their craft. There is bizarre genius here, too, because all about, the results of previous work are on display. The faces are blank, eyes bright yet unseeing; their very existence epitomises perfection, yet their very stillness has propensity to send a shiver down the spine. This is a secret place, sanctuary for clandestine recreation; asylum from a world all too keen to rile. Guilt is sometimes brought here, but it is never entertained long enough for it to stay. Passion for the work makes sure of that—such is the nature of obsession.

Beneath cold light, skill creates objects of desire, delicate deities fashioned in artisan fingers. In contrast, the needlework attaching craftsman's hands to another's wrists are not so refined, yet the dedication behind the stitching is no less omnipotent. Ridged flesh, black stitches, they are a signature to reinvention, rebirth after incomprehensible death.

Despite the thread, blood seeps down the forearms, but it is old; black and foul.

A deed not quite done.

CHAPTER TEN

The Snack Shack Cafe was compact, consisting of no more than twelve tables. The white tablecloths were pristine, and the cutlery gave off sparks under wall-mounted lamps. At the far end of the room, a glass counter held a plethora of sandwiches and pre-toasted paninis, huge freshly baked cookies, and cakes. Behind the display was a serving area with the set menu written up on a blackboard in flamboyant, chalk lettering, served up by the three members of staff, all dressed in smart black t-shirts.

The atmosphere was alive with the chimes of crockery and utensils, the air scented with a blend of coffee and freshly cooked food. Ray and his two colleagues took up a spot at one of the few vacant tables. There was a quiet hubbub about them as patrons discussed the things important to them at that moment in time. Ray recognised a few faces from work and nodded, a passing acknowledgement.

"Okay," he said as the others settled down in their seats. "What are you guys having?"

Mike looked at the menu, a single sheet of beige card he'd plucked from a wooden, slatted stand at the centre of the table. "All day breakfast, please, boss. With extra hash browns and fried bread."

Eloise chuckled. "Didn't you have an all-day breakfast *for* breakfast?"

"I did," Mike admitted. "But yesterday I read an article about embracing other societies. So today, in the spirit of cultural awareness, I'm going full-on Hobbit. This, my dear Eloise, is my *second breakfast.*"

She winked. "And that diet you said you were going to start this week?"

Mike grinned behind his beard. "I'm better at eating than I am at dieting. You just have to follow your nature, right."

"I can't argue with that," Eloise said with a chuckle.

"Okay, okay. I got it, one special," Ray said before addressing Eloise. "What can I get you?"

"Tuna melt, please," she said without hesitation. "And an espresso."

Ray made a mental note of their orders and headed off to the counter. He joined a small queue. Scanning the cafe, his eyes stalled on a man in his fifties who was sitting back in his chair, the remnants of a sandwich on his table, a newspaper opened out, so the headline faced Ray.

Frankenstein Claims More Body-Parts!

Ray took in the words, digested them, and shuddered.

The headline was a reminder that their city had attracted a top-tier sociopath. The tabloid press was having a field day. They'd christened the killer with Mary Shelly's titular doctor after the police confirmed that the MO in the four people murdered so far was that some portion of their body had been taken away as a presumed trophy. No same body part had been taken, so the press jumped on the Frankenstein analogy straight away.

Now people feared that somewhere in the world, a hideous and twisted version of a human being was being assembled to sate whatever monstruous need the killer craved.

His mind had a vague thought about hands stitched to wrists, and he shuddered. Where the hell had *that* come from? Did he just conjure that shit up from nowhere? Deep down, his mind was telling him he'd seen this image before, but he could not connect with it as he would a memory, or a vision, for that matter. This uncertainty left him off kilter. It made him feel vulnerable. He'd watched so many shitty movies in his time, maybe it was from one of those?

"Sir?"

The voice startled him, bringing him back to the here and now. He focused on the implausibly young face staring expectantly at him from behind the glass counter. There was a smile, but the girl's eyes looked harassed.

"Yes, sorry," he said, peering up at the specials board behind her.

Placing his order, he continued to think of just how detached from reality did someone have to be to remove someone's heart while they were still alive.

He didn't have an answer, which he thought as only a good thing

Denise made her way across the car park, hands rummaging around inside her hefty shoulder bag. She eventually retrieved her car keys, which she promptly dropped to the Tarmac. Quietly cursing, she stooped to pick them up, thankful that she'd been lucky enough to find a staff parking space at all. Having thirty pounds per month deducted from her salary for parking guaranteed nothing these days. She'd get better odds on the lottery.

About her, the day was getting dark, the October air brisk and hinting at an impending overnight frost. Her breath steamed out before her, echoing her foggy thoughts of how the day had started off. She could still see the red VW— stark against the hedgerows of her training circuit.

She cussed again, this time inside her head.

She'd never sought out an affair. No doubt, she thought, most people who had been unfaithful at some point in their life had made similar claims. Now, guilt was her companion; the emotions eating away at her, feeding upon her psyche as would some feral, ravenous beast on the carcass of its prey.

Even Ray's seizure at breakfast hadn't been able to shake the image of the white box on the ground in the country lane near their home. Despite the dismissive words to her maverick lover, she'd relented, returning to the spot where her so-called 'gift' had been discarded. She'd found the box containing a ruined, white ball gown, squashed and printed with muddy tyre-tracks. Scooping up the dress and the carton, she'd thrown both into the car boot, the tangible evidence of her infidelity creating guilt far too bright to look upon for too long.

Denise did not have a natural aptitude for betrayal. Over the years, her husband had been dutiful and reliable, a constant in her life. Sure, he had his 'lapses', but more often than not, he made special efforts not to allow these things to impede their life. In this he was selfless, and she knew it.

But she felt that he was also *selfish*. Maybe not consciously, or with malice, but he enjoyed his work, garden, his beer, his books and movies, and little else. She couldn't remember when he'd stopped making sexual advances to her. She'd tried to pinpoint it often enough, but such a thing wasn't conclusive, making her think that it had been a process so insidious, it had somehow become the natural order of things. These days, it was always *she* who initiated such things, usually under the influence of a pinot grigio or six. The sex was little short of serviceable—at least that was how she saw it.

Such a definition was ironic at best given the issues surrounding their inability to conceive children. Her desire for a child—and nature's propensity for spite—was a subject never discussed, like an embarrassing, distant relative.

Yes, they had grieved, becoming angry and seeking comfort in each other, cursing the injustice of such a reality. Denise felt that there was a point where her husband had turned away from the actualities of the situation, as though deciding the time for mourning had passed, succumbing to an ethic where acceptance was the only way forward. This hadn't sat well with her; they'd not even established *why* they could not conceive. Or identified *who* was at—

She'd desperately tried not to think about the situation in terms of 'fault', but sometimes it was difficult to consider things in any other way. Such was the nature of the longing that had made its insatiable presence felt in those early stages.

To her, Ray had succumbed to what *was*, rather than join her in a battle for change, to challenge and close off every avenue before coming to the decision there was nothing more that could be done. This level of apathy from her husband stilted her immediate thoughts of adoption, and somewhere along the way, Denise swallowed her needs in order to maintain the status quo.

Her yearning was to surface from time to time over the following years. She expected nothing less, but as time took its toll on her body, she eventually resigned herself to the inevitable, and her career became her primary focus. She'd become a clinician of local renown, and, as a consultant midwife, a national profile was to follow, the exposure offering her great recognition.

Her professional esteem took her onto the conference circuit, presentations and keynote speeches allowing her opportunity to spread the word about the projects and developments that furthered modern midwifery. Projects that made a *difference*.

It was at one of these conferences that she met the man that she was to sleep with several times. The transition from professional interest to carnal desire was cultivated over a period of eight months. There had been a Quality Improvement (QI) initiative established by the NHS Improvement Scheme (NHSI), and Denise had managed to procure funds to take a team on a course to enable them to design, develop and roll out a QI initiative in their service. On top of the day job, it had been heavy work, but worth it in terms of experience and the service improvements she and her team had established in the process.

The course had been spread out—three events, each four days in duration, twelve days in total. The first had been held in Leeds, the next in Manchester, and it was on the third—which ended in a gala ball—that had seen her go up to her hotel room with one of the programme's lead facilitators.

Peter Cound was in his mid-fifties, a project coordinator with NHSI, and had been facilitating every event Denise had attended. He had given praise, he'd demonstrated a passion for her thoughts and ideas—remaining in contact via telephone calls and Zoom chats, just to make sure their projects were on track for presentation on the final course—and, above all, he *listened*: at the events, or on the phone, and finally, on the last night, where they had sat in a bar and talked until the early hours about their pasts and plans for the future.

When he'd talked about his grown-up son and daughter from a failed marriage, Denise had suddenly become upset, prompting Peter to place a comforting hand on her knee. Whether it was the moment or the booze, they had kissed, and the offer of continuing their discussion in her room was out of her mouth soon after. Hand in hand they entered the elevator, he in his tuxedo, she in that damn white ball gown that was about to become a symbol of infidelity. Despite her guilt, she still shivered when she thought of him slowly teasing the delicate lace bodice away from her trembling body.

The sex was incredible. Being with someone different made her feel alive, and it allowed her to be more liberal. Her lover's tastes were exotic, to say the least, and she revelled in new experiences. After years of being in control, it was refreshing to be at the mercy of someone else, someone who sought only to fulfil her desires.

That was the start of it all. The guilt was to come much later.

Like in that moment, for example, when the thought of those nights crossed Denise's mind as she stood back up after retrieving her keys from the ground. It came as a wave, not helped, of course, by Peter's visit in the country lane that morning. But at that point, guilt was also mingled with anger and fear. Anger that he would dare do such a thing, fear of the implications should her husband ever find out.

Because, even now, she knew that no matter how much fun she'd had with Peter, she'd never had any intention to ever leave her husband. She valued loyalty more than anything else. She knew some would argue that infidelity and betrayal were the very nemeses of such tenets. In part, she would've agreed, but *true* loyalty lay in the heart, and she had no love for Peter Cound. Yes, she had lust and the thrill of the game, but that was something she knew would ultimately wane.

Peter knew it too—that was clear from his first 'gift'. The gown was a statement, a display of how much he wanted to rekindle their initial tryst, the consummate wanton passion of it all. Denise sensed desperation in the act, the behaviour of someone clinging to something precious, yet precarious. The rash attempt to kiss her that morning was even more evidence of an escalation in his reckless behaviour.

But she was equally as resolute in her decision that the time for this to end was upon them both. All Peter had to do was listen to what she was telling him, that this was over, and over for good.

She held her breath and took stock of the moment, the thoughts whirling about her brain, making her feel dizzy. After a pause, she made her way to her vehicle, the cold spurring her on.

It was only as she approached the car did her pace slow, eventually stalling as she looked at the object lying across the bonnet of her silver Audi A4.

The long, thin box had no logos or lettering. It was made out of material similar to a carton, and she prodded it with a tentative finger, as if afraid it might explode. After a moment, she placed her bag on the Audi's bonnet and picked up the box, pulling off the lid and peering inside.

There, lying on a bed of velvet, were twin-braided thongs of fine leather. There was also a sliver of paper secured to the inside of the lid. On the paper were three words:

Your second gift.

"For fuck's sake," she muttered.

CHAPTER ELEVEN

THE interior of Birmingham New Street Grand Central Station was made up of a series of high, interconnected archways, interspersed with ceilings of curved panes of glass, giving it the look and feel of an airport. The main concourse was oval, its perimeter lined by two floors of shopping arcades and restaurants, their facades an enticing mix of colourful banners and glittering displays. On a good day, over 127,000 passengers would pass through the station, linking it to all major cities in the UK.

During rush hour, the wide corridors acted as tributaries, syphoning commuters to the twelve platforms, accessed by escalators and adjacent staircases made from dulled steel. It was a *twenty-four hour, seven days a week* kind of place. From those heading off to work, to revellers coming into the city for a night out, to the homeless brave enough to venture away from New Street itself to risk sleeping inside until the security staff moved them on, the station saw all walks of life, be they work commuters or tourists, the latter often stopping on the ground floor to take pictures with 'Ozzy'—a thirty-three foot, two and a half tonne semi-mechanoid bull, named after fellow *Brummie* and Black Sabbath legend, Ozzy Osbourne.

Ray preferred the train journey home. Not because it meant work was done for the day—most evenings he would complete commissioner reports or outstanding risk assessments that would ultimately inform Board papers, while Denise saw to her own paperwork. No, he preferred the joys of the Flexible Return Ticket because it meant that he could wait until the rush hour had finished before heading back to the village.

Even at this time, the place was still busy, though not to the extent where he'd have to stand for most of the journey once he'd boarded the train. He knew that by the time it hit Longbridge—a station several stops down the line—the carriages would be pretty much empty, save for those few who were heading home to the Worcestershire town of Redditch six miles hence.

He waited on the platform, collar turned up against the chill blowing through the tunnel leading off northeast, and considered the nuances of his day, sifting through events, filing them for later that evening, when he and Denise would have their inevitable work-day debrief. He would omit the hideous images he'd seen on the train that morning, of course. And his remonstrations with 'track-suit guy' outside the station. Those discussions wouldn't feature, because they *never* did.

Sometimes he wondered how he'd been able to hoodwink his wife for so long, putting it down to a well-established façade he'd cultivated in his youth. He wasn't proud of such an accomplishment. Lying to someone was not often associated with integrity, especially when that 'someone' was a person you supposedly loved. Still, the wall he'd built growing up was the only thing that he truly understood. It had allowed him to hide his ability ever since those first episodes, meaning that he could at least pretend to be normal, and in doing so reap the rewards denied to those stigmatised by derogatory or medicalised labels. He thought about his earlier con-clusion as to how times and language had changed. But tolerance remained a fickle beast. These days, terms such as *neurodivergent* cer-tainly softened the edges, but for those determined enough, bigotry remained steadfast.

Back in his teens, the concept of madness, and the fickle atti-tude society held towards it, did not feature in his decision-making process. As a teenager, all he wanted to make sure of was he didn't give his peers any more ammunition to take the piss. It was bad enough that he'd been hospitalised by his own stupidity, and that was not a tale that went away fast, remaining the stuff of school comedy legend for years to come.

So, he'd concocted the story that he suffered from epilepsy, brought on by his head trauma—not far-fetched by any means. As a tale, it had the upshot of killing two birds with one stone, the irony of such a metaphor never lost on him. Sure, it wasn't as sophisticated as the diagnosis he would steal from the internet many years later, but it enabled him to pass off his lapses as seizures of a sort, and ultimately stopped his peers from teasing him. And, as time marched on, his friends came to see him as someone to protect from the ills of school life. Looking back, he wasn't proud to become dependent on them, but at the time, a kid who was different had to do what they needed in order to get by. He doubted that things had changed since then, especially when he saw the tragic statistics for Child and Adolescent Mental Health Services. A dearth of beds and practitioners, the alarming suicide rates—there was a crisis running rampant through the healthcare system, and so far, no one had any idea of how to arrest the situation, let alone stop it. He felt for these kids, currently out of kilter with the world. He *understood* them. No, it wasn't exactly the same—he got that—but the sense of being an 'oddity' in a world so absorbed with aesthetics. Something had to give when a person couldn't find the means to fit in.

He was lucky. He'd found a way to hide. Epilepsy was the ruse he took with him through life, including his relationship with Denise. She was understanding, and the guilt at duping her bit deep in those early days. Now, each time he lied about his condition, Ray was left with a dull ache, like that of an arthritic joint during a cold spell.

This was, of course, far more acceptable than telling Denise the truth. He wasn't quite sure how painful it would be to see the disbelief—the incredulity—in her eyes if he ever told her about the visions. Every time he thought about it—and he had done so on more occasions than he could count—his heart would judder in his chest, and his breath would stutter in his throat.

No, blissful ignorance was the order of the day, and he would follow it to the letter. He had so much to lose, and so little to gain by coming clean. That wasn't to say that there had not been times when he'd been in such despair at not being able to talk to anyone about it. Those were the moments where he'd sought out forums on the internet, seeking succour and understanding but finding only spurious advice and the paranoic ramblings of conspiracy theorists.

His search for cyber-solace was short-lived; he'd bailed within a month. Instead, he sought diversions, gardening becoming a prominent weapon in his arsenal as he battled against despair. Denise had teased him about becoming an old man before his time. The dig had been playful, but he sometimes wondered if the anxieties of life were finally leaving their mark on him.

Still, he'd converted the bottom of the garden into a small allotment. Denise wasn't a fan, but the waiting list for a local plot was ridiculous. Besides, the one area of gardening he didn't enjoy was mowing; getting rid of a third of the lawn and replacing it with a vegetable patch was a no-brainer when it came to the early days of laying out his garden.

In winter, he grew cabbages, parsnips and leeks, planting seedlings earlier in the year to maximise the crop, using fleeces and straw to protect them from frost. In August, he'd transfer seed potatoes to the ground, ready for a crop ready to harvest at Christmas. He also had a reasonably sized greenhouse, and there he grew tomatoes, cucumbers and asparagus.

All in all, the advanced planning and rotational nature of gardening fed into his natural ability to follow process. And, what was more, he *loved* doing it.

He smiled as he thought of his garden and the peace it brought to his life, especially when standing on train station platforms. After ten minutes, the train arrived, and on time. He boarded it, his mind on the more practical tasks of prepping the ground for spring.

Who knew that you'd get so much out of a pastime requiring so much foresight, his mind mused.

The engine pulled off and he enjoyed his seat. The carriage had several other commuters, many of them hunkered down with their smartphones, scanning screens or listening through headphones.

A woman in her twenties sat hunched over a table seat, tapping an iPad as though her life depended on it. Her legs jutted out into the aisle, the lithe limbs clad in black tracksuit pants, her feet—crossed at the ankles—fashioned in expensive training shoes. The attire made Ray think of the guy who accosted him outside the station that morning.

No, that wasn't quite right. The thought made him think about *how* the guy had responded to Ray's instruction to let go of his arm, like he'd had no choice but to do it. As always, Ray toyed with the idea that such things were improbable, but then he considered his other abilities, and toned down his scepticism.

The element that helped him to embrace such a thing was his recollection of how it felt at the time, the sensation of the thought slipping out of his mind as he'd said the words, how they'd became a command, impossible to resist. One thing was for certain—this kind of thing was new. Somehow, it left him more uneasy than the ability to witness hideously traumatic events before they happened. He was pulled from his uneasy thoughts by raucous laughter.

Another passenger, a guy in a creased grey suit, chatted amiably but loudly, phone wedged between his ear and his shoulder as he rifled through some paperwork in his lap.

There's always one, Ray thought as he looked up at the 'Quiet Zone' sign by the carriage ventilation window. Denise's jibe about becoming old before his time made Ray mind his own business for a while.

Shhhhh!

The hiss was so harsh it made Ray jump, a small cry escaping his lips. He looked about him, the other passengers remaining fixated on their devices, apparently unaware. He gave a furtive glance to the man on the phone, and the woman with the iPad, and then looked back down the carriage. Nothing appeared untoward. Outside the window, the train was leaving the platform behind. Within a few moments, they would enter the mile-long tunnel that would take them out of the station.

For some reason, the thought of darkness beyond the window

left him nervous. Things sometimes lurked in the dark after all, didn't they?

Shhhh!

"What the hell *is* that?"

His words were loud in the carriage, and a few seconds later the train hit the tunnel, the windows turning to black slabs in which the only thing he could see was his own startled reflection.

He was thankful that the overhead lights remained; he wasn't sure just how he'd cope if the world suddenly went completely dark. The thought made him shiver.

It was as he considered this fear that his thought became a reality, and the carriage was plunged into darkness.

He opened his mouth and screamed long and hard, but nothing came out. Around him, he could sense movement; things skulked through the carriage, shapes that defied definition.

Shhh!

The sound came again, this time longer, and more pronounced. Even in his terror, he thought he recognised it as bursts of static. Numbed by horror, his mind still tried to make sense of it all, tried to keep his focus on the fact this was some kind of vision—a bad vision, worse than anything else he'd ever witnessed—but a vision all the same.

More sounds now, the creaking and squeaking of the things that seemed to be moving through the carriage, emerging and separating from the shadows.

They looked humanoid, yet devoid of any features. Hyphened mouths and glittering silver eyes reflected the meagre half-light, and their bodies seemed clad in garb as black as tar, a flickering light—akin to a sputtering candle—drawing lines of sickly yellow across the surface. All over their bodies were stitches, the needlework haphazard, the ugliness made oddly beautiful as it turned to silver under the wavering light.

A dull thud came into the mix, a slow pulse that seemed to reverberate through the carriage and into his brain. Something else accompanied it—synthesised chords and ghastly chants in a language he did not understand.

A shape stood over him, silver-slit eyes looming. "Look at what I have become," it said with a drawn-out hiss. "Chaos and order will make us whole again."

Ray tried to move backwards, as though the seat could somehow absorb him the way a sponge soaks up water. The shape moved ever closer, and no matter how much he tried, Ray could not pull his eyes away from it. A featureless face loomed into his and the air reeked of sickly sweet berries and plastic. He gagged and pushed himself further into his seat. The familiar laughter came, turning his heart to ice water.

"Come. Embrace us."

More movement—to his right. He turned his head, trying to catch sight of the latest thing bent on taunting him, but before his eyes could achieve focus, the image shifted, fast; a smear in the air, and he had to seek it out again, failing every time.

"Your paramour calls to you," the elusive shape teased. "Do you not hear?"

Ray risked looking about him, his sense of hope seemingly pathetic. "Denise?"

"No. The abyss."

Without warning, Ray felt the oppressive darkness ooze into the periphery of his vision, and with it an image, a great amorphous shape, pulsating like thunderheads touched by lightning. He recognised it as the image he'd seen in the station windows that very morning. This time, the shape harnessed swathes of grief and loss and guilt, so potent they made Ray weep.

"This is the world as you have known it," the nebulous mass crooned. "Would you have dominion over it? Would you be its saviour, its *master*?"

The rhetoric reverberated about him, through him. "Who are you?" Ray whispered. "*What* are you?"

"A guide."

"To where?" Ray said.

"Your purpose."

"I don't understand."

"You will."

Without warning, the lights came back, and Ray slapped a hand over his mouth to stop himself screaming out in relief.

The tunnel was gone, the passengers—back again.

A figure still stood beside him though, a disgruntled conductor who stared down at him with a steely expression of intolerance.

"So, are you going to show me your ticket or carry on staring at me all night like I've got two heads?"

Ruffled, Ray sat up and tried to regain his composure. "Yes, of course. Sorry."

He handed over his ticket, his rebellious fingers almost dropping it twice en route.

Through walls of glass, he watches—unseen—the woman of his dreams, hem of white linen, a wake of foaming sea. Her movements are languid and light, a dance of life gracing the very air through which she passes. Oh, how he longs to be her suitor, take her by the hand as Strauss' Blue Danube strokes the air, rising and falling, swelling and swirling, the cadence of passion.

His heart aches, a profound yearning made worse by the nagging reality of unrequited love. It brings bright anger, the crystal walls trembling as though such ire is an entity in itself, threatening to shatter this beautiful yet brittle world that has been created just for this finely nuanced fantasy. He turns to place a palm against a mirrored partition, but there is horror and confusion; the face reflected in the glass has no eyes, just deep, crimson sockets and bloody tears gushing down pallid cheeks. Yet he can still see his mouth open to scream, the bloody face in the mirror, a facsimile. His cry turns the walls to shards as this castle of glass smashes under the hammer of reality, and he comforts himself in knowing that very soon all will be dark, and he will hurt no more.

CHAPTER TWELVE

"Thought you were out tonight?"

Ray leaned against the kitchen counter with a glass of merlot in his hand. He swirled the dark red liquid and tried not to think of hot blood and gutted abdomens.

Denise walked into the kitchen and placed her bag in the corner of the breakfast bar.

"Amy bailed. Said she had a headache, but I suspect she'd got a better offer." She nodded to his wine glass. "Got one of those for me?"

"Always."

He retrieved another glass from one of the kitchen's many high cupboards. The shimmer of crystal had him suddenly thinking of a face with empty eye sockets, soundlessly screaming in despair. He pulled in a breath and pushed the image away.

Fuck all this stress and fuck these intrusive thoughts. Maybe he needed a few more glasses of wine than usual this evening, just to dull the senses. He could even try to encourage Denise to take his mind off things for a while. It had been some time since they had slept together. In fact, he couldn't *remember* the last time. A month? Two?

He placed the glass on the counter. "You eaten?"

"Not hungry."

He poured her a drink and handed the wine to her. As she took it, her eyes flitted to his face. For a scant second, Ray thought he saw something in her eyes, a sadness that was gone as soon as it came. He'd seen the same look that morning as he'd emerged from the bathroom. The recollection unsettled him more than thoughts of people with no eyes in their sockets.

As she pulled her work mobile from the pocket of her coat to put it in her bag, he made another observation.

"You know you've lost an earring?"

Her hands went to her lobes. The one on the right was bare. Panicked, her mind conjured up the memory of Peter grabbing hold of her that morning. "Damn it."

He sighed, sadly. "Your favourite diamond studs."

They were a gift, brought back from Cape Town, South Africa when he'd presented at a conference in the 90s. The look on her face was a mix of confusion and, for a moment, sudden anxiety. Then, just as before, it was gone.

"You okay?"

Her response was brittle. "No. I love these earrings. Hopefully someone has found it at work. Don't make me feel any worse than I already do."

"Sorry." It sounded lame, so he thought he could try and save it. "Maybe we could go to that movie instead?"

She headed for the kitchen door. "It would have already started. Besides, I'm tired. I'll go and take a bath and watch some catch-up TV."

"I could always come and wash your back?"

He eyed him for a few seconds. "Don't make promises you can't keep."

"Happy to keep this one."

But she'd already left the room, and if his words had reached her, she didn't acknowledge it.

It was the dogma of present times.

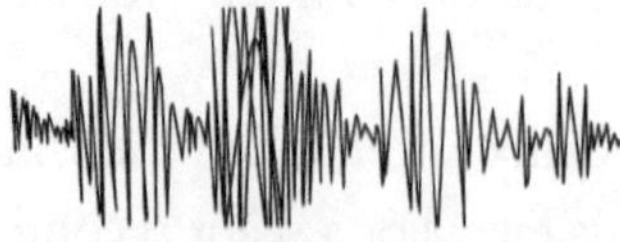

Denise reclined in the bath, warm water and crackling bubbles soothing her taut muscles. She tried to relax, but her mind was working overtime as she recalled the card she'd found with the leather thongs. And the three words in Peter's fine script:

Your second gift.

She'd stowed the card and the thongs alongside the grubby white gown in the tyre compartment of her Audi, all the time wondered where this was going. Ambiguity was currently the order of the day. She couldn't remember a time when she'd been so conflicted.

Now that damn earring had been lost.

Amongst the suds, she tentatively texted Peter, his phone number stored under the assumed name of Carla Smith in her contacts.

Hi Carla! I lost an earring the last time we met up. Can you look for it and let me know if you find it, pls?

Her phone buzzed almost immediately. Shit, was this guy sitting on his damn phone?

No problem, my love. Peter x

She cursed under her breath and deleted the text thread. He'd been told not to use incriminating terms of endearment, and certainly not his real fucking name!

Jesus. How the hell had she got herself into this mess?

She splashed warm water on her face, but it provided no more clarity. Things were twisted and life was no longer pedestrian. For as long as she could remember, this kind of excitement was what she'd craved, albeit in a never-going-to-happen kind of way.

Now she was trying to end an affair as her husband tended to his vegetable patch and her obstinate ex-beau was finding it hard to take 'it's over' for an answer. There was a resentment building within her, aimed squarely at Peter. He thought control was all part of her connection with him, and while it had been exciting buying into a period of wanton lust, it was now seriously starting to piss her off. He had no right to turn up only a mile from her home, trying to force himself upon her. He had no right to ignore her wish for all of this to end.

But with the anger came that quiet fear. She didn't know where the fuck it was all going, or how far Peter would go to continue the affair, what he was happy to destroy. His reckless text messages were part of his reluctance to accept the reality of things. In the pit of her stomach, reality nestled. She was becoming scared of Peter and what he was bringing into her life. This simply wasn't fun anymore.

She needed it to end. She needed her life back.

With a deep breath she slipped beneath the water, happy to drown out the world for a while.

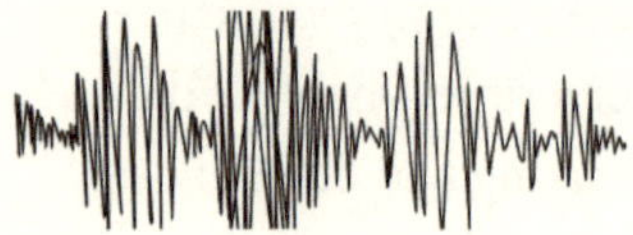

The funeral parlour is heavily scented with fuchsias. She knows that these are her father's favourites because she would always see vases full of the bell-shaped petals—vibrant purples and reds—on the windowsill or on the sideboard of their home. Part of her knows that this is a blend of dream and reality. Another part knows that it is an event that has made her the person she is now.

A twin quad of chairs creates a centre aisle leading up to a stage where a mahogany coffin shimmers under the overhead lights. One half of the coffin is open; the lining is pearl-white, and appears to give off a radiance all of its own.

In her stomach, Eloise feels a heady mix of sadness and fear. She is holding onto the hand of Tiffany, and her concerned eyes meet the kind yet heart-broken gaze of her mother.

"Are you okay, Mum?"

Tiffany merely gives her a wan smile. There are tears twinkling in her eyes. Eloise can see the vestiges of grief on her mother's own face, the way her eyes are red and puffy from her secret bouts of tears. She hears her mother at night when she thinks Eloise is asleep. The sobs come like tiny coughs, and Eloise knows her mother is trying to mute them with a pillow.

She says nothing and grips her mother's hand as they walk down the aisle towards the stage, towards the coffin. Eloise's heart still thumps in her chest, and her legs feel as though they are turning to useless cylinders of rubber.

Both women flinch at a sudden voice behind them. Eloise turns along with her mother, quickly seeing her Aunt Molly, a kind woman who works as a care assistant in a local nursing home. She is dressed in black, waving for Eloise's mother to come to her.

"I need to talk to Aunt Molly," Tiffany says before letting go of her hand and heading off.

Eloise does not think that she will ever feel so alone again.

The sensation almost crushes her. For reasons she cannot explain, she does not stay put. Nor does she follow her mother. Instead, she heads off to the coffin, where her dear father is now laid to rest in his best suit made from blue velvet. She mounts the steps to the stage, the heavily patterned carpet muting her footsteps, and stands, looking down upon him.

His hair is grey-white, his hairline receded. In life, he would have had a beaming smile, made brighter by his gold incisor. Now he looks as though he is sleeping, his skin smooth and unblemished, with a sheen on his brow and cheeks. Deep inside her mind there is a flicker-flash of insight that tells her that in some ways her father's face looks artificial—as if he is wearing a mask, the kind of mask that people wear at masquerades she has seen in period dramas on the TV.

Eloise's eyes scan the inert body, and she can see that the blue and black striped tie is slightly askew, exposing a crisp white shirt. She instinctively feels the need to put the tie straight, just as she'd seen her father do on countless occasions before going to church.

As she makes contact with the smooth material, she is overcome by a great sense of love that leaves her breathless. As she steadies herself, her palm makes contact with her father's abdomen. She can feel something there, something ridged and rigid. Her trembling finger pushes the tie aside to expose his shirt buttons, not quite flat against his dead stomach.

Inquisitive fingers tentatively trace an outline, a horizontal line that is jagged against her fingertips. She pops open a button and peers beneath, the scent of embalming fluid strong in her nose. Her eyes mist and a tear falls with a small tapping sound. It seeps into his shirt as though needing to be part of him, and somewhere far away, she hears a sob and realises that her grief has found form...

CHAPTER THIRTEEN

Eloise woke, her pillow wet with tears, the dream vivid enough to leave its mark. She wiped the dampness from her eyes and cheeks, reaching over to the bedside cupboard for the glass of water she usually brought up to bed with her.

Sluggish fingers and blurred eyes did their work, and she knocked the glass over. The contents may have been lukewarm on her wrist, but her response was as if she'd been scalded.

"Shit!"

Suddenly awake and jumping up, she set the glass upright and looked at the rivulets as they ran down the cupboard, creating three tiny pools of water on the hardwood floor.

She pulled on her white, laced dressing gown and padded downstairs, heading for the kitchen where a large roll of paper towel waited on the grey work counter. At the bottom of the stairs she went left, crossing the small lounge, her palm tracing along the back of the sofa. The lounge was at the back of the house, walls painted lilac, the skirting boards white. When she wasn't dreaming of her dead father and jumping up in the middle of the night, the fresh and airy tones made her feel relaxed.

But the lounge was by no means her favourite room in the house. That honour went to the conservatory, a place with a large beech wood dining table, flanked by leather chairs and a corner seat sofa of soft brown leather. Vertical blinds covered windows that looked out upon a large lawn edged by flower beds, with a great willow tree standing proud in the middle. In the summer, all of the blinds would be thrown wide. In the winter, with the darkness outside pressing against the glass, the slats would be adjusted at twilight.

In the kitchen, Eloise went to the roll of kitchen towel but pulled up short. She had a sudden craving for a decaff latte. No surprise, as this was her usual treat when the dreams robbed her of sleep.

The minor spillage upstairs was now forgotten as she busied herself with her De'Longhi coffee maker, the cough and gurgle of the froth enhancer loud in the galley kitchen. She finished up making her drink, taking a sip from the tall latte glass, and walked through a set of opened double doors to the left of the silver fridge-freezer, leading off to the conservatory.

Beyond the glass, the moon was high, the hedges and trees lining her garden boundary monochrome. At the bottom of the lawn, she could make out the shape of the pergola. In the height of summer, she would often head down to the covered structure and sit at the table there, eating fresh salads during the week, a takeaway or two over the weekends. The spot reminded her of Tiffany and the many discussions they'd had sat under the awning, glasses of chilled prosecco helping everything make sense.

Even as she looked at the table, Eloise fancied she could see a shape standing in the deep shadow, and was comforted by the thought that it was a fanciful image of her mother.

But even as she looked upon the shadow, she felt that something about it was off.

Then, it moved.

Eloise stepped away from the window, a cry stuck fast in her throat. Instinctively, her hand went to her dressing gown pocket, quickly realizing her phone was on charge by her bed. She calmed herself with rational thought.

There's no one there, her mind said. *It's a trick of the light because you're thinking about Mom and dreaming about Dad.* She waited for a few more moments, moving closer to the window. Sure enough, the pergola was empty. Save for the table and chairs, nothing untoward lurked in the shadows.

Still, she double-checked the lock on the conservatory door, and then did a circuit of the house to make sure all the windows and doors were secure.

Once this was complete, she went back up to her bedroom, circling through the kitchen to grab the kitchen roll.

Upstairs, she mopped up the water on the floor and climbed into bed. Even though she was sure she'd just mitigated a non-existent risk, Eloise lay in bed awake for what seemed an age, listening for any creaks or signs of movement.

Better safe than sorry wasn't written in any Health and Safety legislation, but it was a mandate Eloise had always lived by, and she had no intention of deviating from its injunction tonight.

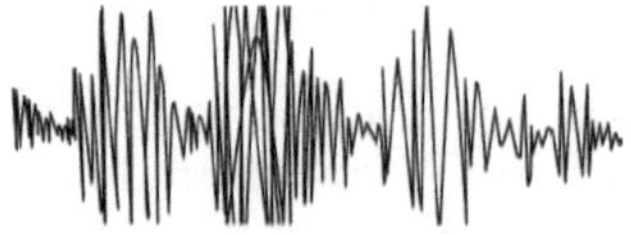

From the safety of the garden shed, the figure had watched the woman close the blinds earlier that evening. It was a waiting game, and usually the stakeout was a painstakingly cautious affair.

In the time the person had stood there staring at the house, the thought of the woman lying in bed in skimpy pyjamas or, even better, naked—save for a pair of panties—had been the single focus. There was even the consideration of whether she masturbated before she went to sleep. Such thoughts created their own special sensations, of course.

The thrill that she'd come back down and looked directly at this very spot was exhilarating. The flow of her dressing gown adding an extra lift to an already outlandish, dangerous fantasy. But being seen was never on the agenda, a momentary lapse of judgement that had potential to end things before they had a chance to come to fruition. Carelessness was the nemesis of patience.

Still, it had been a close call, but the secret remained safe. It was all about getting back perspective. Yes, this was a process that was driven by intense desire, but it was also important to remain resolute and cautious, the tools of a steadfast predator.

For now, there had to be contentment in the fact that the woman had come to the window, and she could be seen for the briefest of moments. This event now played out over and over as eyes remained fixed on the conservatory windows, while hands sought out ways to add pleasure to the ritual.

CHAPTER FOURTEEN

ABOUT him the world is dark, an oppressive nothingness that has him feeling as though he has simply ceased to exist, save for his consciousness and the ever present understanding that this place belongs to another. He is entombed, a silent witness, drifting through events like flotsam at the mercy of the ocean's pull. More sensations, that of rising through this inky netherworld, the movement known only by the touch of a breeze on his unseen face, and during this ascent, he espies something alien way above him, a circle of light, like that of a star dimmed by a skein of cloud, slowly growing in diameter as the distance closes, until there is no darkness, only an orb, its circumference jagged, the edges, grey.

There is movement beyond this orbital fascia, a writhing mass of white flesh and angular limbs, slick with moisture, juxtaposed by growls and whimpers. He can see this indistinguishable mass cavorting on a landscape of twisted linen, the room dingy with tired, aged furniture. The scene is abstract, surreal, enough to tell him that this is another vision, but the level of ambiguity is in danger of crushing his mind until another sensation takes over, one that has potency. The sight in the circle is making him aroused. He likes the way the shape bucks and thrusts, the sounds that echo about him, sighs and screams and nonstop chants.

"Yes. Yes. Yes."

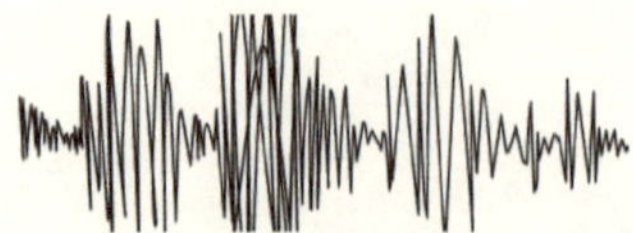

Eloise finished up the report and saved it for one final read through. With a stretch of lissom limbs, she let go a sigh and reached for her disposable mug of coffee she'd bought from the cafeteria, left neglected in favour of completing the document on her screen. She drained the tepid liquid with delicate gusto.

The previous night's events had left her feeling somewhat out of sorts in that most of her dream wasn't a dream at all—it was *recollection*. Enough to have her waking with tears and laughter, the emotional ambiguity leaving a residue over breakfast as she came to terms with it all.

She figured it hadn't been helped by her mind playing tricks on her when she'd looked out on the garden, thinking someone had been standing there, watching. The sensation that passed through her was no longer that of anxiety. It had become a muted anger that made her shiver like a cold draft on her neck.

"You done with that cup, Ellie?"

At the sound of the reedy voice, Eloise felt a shudder pass through her body. Looking up, she saw Brendan Short scuttling towards her with a black plastic refuse sack.

Brendan was a small man in his late fifties. He had thin, grey hair that shimmered with grease, and his paunch and 'moobs' stood proudly under his taut crimson tee-shirt like a bloody mountain range.

Eloise had no cause to feel revulsion whenever the domestic worker came to empty the bins and clear away litter accumulated during the day. Her parents would've scalded her at such prejudice, and they would have been right to do so. He'd never done her any harm after all, and she felt guilty about how she reacted to him. When she told herself that it was instinctual and she had no grounds for her behaviour, her mind would push back to remind her that instincts were there for a reason, an innate security feature hotwired into the primordial brain in order to foster a climate of survival.

Despite all of this. she still had reservations about how his watery, cold blue eyes considered her, the way he never appeared to blink whenever he spoke, his stare seemingly eating beneath her clothes, her skin, into her very soul. Again, she shivered inside, trying not to gawk at the raised nubs on his chest where his nipples pressed against the confines of his tee-shirt.

Brendan pulled his mouth into a smile. He had a dark stain on his lips, and Eloise shut down thoughts of his mouth attempting to press against hers.

"You okay?" he said.

She attempted to inject some neutrality into her tone. "Yes. Just busy, that's all."

The smile stayed in place, as though his face had forgotten how it worked. "I guess that's why they pay us, right?"

She nodded, not really wanting to become embroiled in a conversation. As though fate decided to take pity on her, the phone on her desk rang. She snatched up the receiver almost immediately, handing Brendan the spent coffee mug with her free hand as, in her ear, the voice of a woman from the governance team requested detail on a recent dataset presented to the local commissioning group.

He took the carton from her, his fingers brushing lightly against hers for a nanosecond. The disgust was powerful and lingering, forcing her to turn away from him slightly, using the pretence of the phone call to end any further dialogue.

I'm sure he's meant to wear gloves, she told herself. The impulse to go to the bathroom and scour her fingers clean with anti-bacterial scrub was overpowering. *This is what it must be like to suffer with Obsessive Compulsive Disorders*, she thought as she engaged with the caller. As the voice on the phone droned on, Eloise thought she'd have to read up on ritualistic behaviours, just to be sure.

During these moments, she sensed Brendan walking away. She looked back briefly to check, and the domestic was indeed moving towards Mike's cluttered desk. He stooped to empty the wastebasket next to the vacant workstation and suddenly peered back at her, eyes bright and relentless in their intensity.

Eloise gave him a token wave and returned back to her call, the faux smile on her face slipping away as soon as Brendan was unable to see her do it.

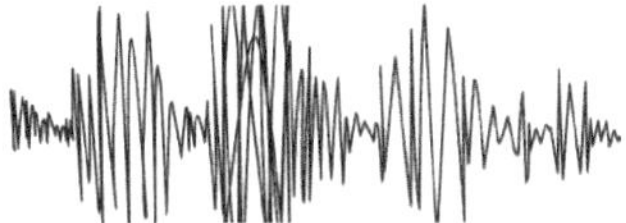

Brendan shuffled through the aisle made from the many workstations on the mezzanine. He pushed his trolley ahead of him, the twin tiers laden with cleaning products and disposable cloths.

As he passed through, his keen eyes alighted upon the various figures working away behind their desks or standing chatting, folders and files in hand. Inside, he relished the clandestine pleasure he felt at a glimpse of a bare thigh, skirts hitched slightly too high, or the sheer excitement when a woman stooped for her bag and her ill-fitting blouse revealed the swell of a breast. These were small things, but they were a luxury to Brendan, his acute brain making note of every detail in a split second.

The most interesting part was the ease in which he could covet the tiny pleasures on show all about him. Part of it was down to caution cultivated over time, yet the lion's share came from his job. For all intents and purposes, he was invisible to those about him, just an inconsequential shadow who drifted through the lives of his colleagues. And in this obscure netherworld, Brendan cruised like a hungry shark, senses homing in on his unsuspecting prey.

He enjoyed the freedom anonymity brought to him. But just now, when he realised that Eloise had sensed him watching her, a thrill passed through him that had left him dizzy; the knowledge that she suspected his attention was far more powerful, intoxicating. There was another factor—something new—in the reaction he thought he'd seen in Eloise's eyes, a flicker of revulsion. But rather than being stalled with rejection, Brendan had felt a powerful thrill pass through him. Eloise *knew* he was watching her and had responded. Holding such emotional influence over another made him feel omnipotent, no matter how fleeting the moment had been.

Now all he wanted to do was to make sure he could engineer such moments again.

And soon.

CHAPTER FIFTEEN

In the bathrooms of Trust HQ, Ray was washing his hands. Four toilet cubicles were reflected in the mirrors above the sink units, pale grey doors thrown wide, and the twin urinals on the adjacent wall, unoccupied. The slosh from the faucet echoed about the open space as Ray allowed the water to fill his cupped hands, planting his face into them. Despite his unsettled nerves, he relished the immediate coolness on his cheeks and eyelids.

The flutter in his guts reminded him that he was slightly nervous. In fifteen minutes, he was due to present at the Trust Clinical Governance Committee, and the quivering sensation in his stomach was par for the course. Public speaking was something that had never come easy to him, and if he had the choice, he'd never volunteer. However, his role demanded that he did so on at least a few occasions per month, and while he never got used to it, he *did* know the material he was presenting—enthused over it, even—and that pretty much helped steer him through times such as these.

To ease the tension from his neck muscles he looked up. The lights encased in their circular housing were dull discs, suns trying to burn through dense cloud. The image unexpectedly made him think of writhing limbs as his groin stirred.

"For Christ's sake, Ray," he muttered. "Get a damn grip on this shit."

These intrusive thoughts were getting to be a concern. As if he didn't have enough to contend with. He knew all about how the mind sometimes tried to usurp someone while under stress, an insidious assault of negativity determined to undermine self-esteem until the sufferer doubted their own morality. This was a symptom he hadn't considered when he'd made the decision that, for now at least, he was going to stop trying to understand his recent visions and their potential implications. On the surface, he'd convinced himself that such a conclusion related to being focused on work.

This was not the entire story, of course.

The content of the visions were disconcerting enough. The fact that he was now *interacting* with the hideous characters contained within them—and was seemingly able to somehow compel the corporeal when he felt threatened—also meant he had no choice but to accept that the nature of his abilities was *changing*. As always, he tried to ground such events, no matter how fantastic they appeared. This also meant pondering some potential unsavoury causes.

For instance, perhaps it meant whatever damage his brain had sustained all those years ago was getting worse. Or perhaps he'd managed to bag himself a tumour, just for good measure. Such fleeting, disturbing notions were potentially indicative that he preferred a psychological, rather than a neurological, reason for these changes. The former could be fixed; the latter, well, not always. Part of him thought it just dessert—he'd pretty much invited it, after all, claiming neurological illness, tempting fate. Maybe this was karma, and the abyss had heard his call, mistaking it for a want.

This didn't explain everything, and there was a very real chance that, if he delved too deeply into such affairs, such actions would ultimately fail to give credible answers to *anything at all*. The idea that all of this was beyond his control, the sense that he was being manipulated by powers way beyond his understanding, was never far from his mind, and that terrified him.

Indeed, his heart quickened, and he chastised himself for allowing his mind to drift back to the very topic he'd sworn to avoid that day. It mattered not. Within moments, and without warning, Ray *was* reminded of just how much control he had over his latent curse.

Because the world changed.

The very air seemed to vibrate, the scene ahead wavering as

though he was looking through a wall of great, rising heat. The sky overhead was bloodshot, and the clouds were a combination of vile, gory smears and streaks. Writhing, bulbous plants oscillated at his feet, their teardrop forms billowing and collapsing like a runner's lungs at the finish line, the surface mottled with great dribbling boils, making his stomach churn.

Not real, he screamed inside his head. *All of this is just bullshit.*

The ground was thick red grass, and his feet were deep in the blades, making him feel as though he was standing on a giant, slurping tongue that waited to suck him down the gullet of a great beast. Despite doubting the validity of what he was experiencing, Ray felt rising panic.

He found that he was being pulled towards the horizon, an impossible premise, yet one that he accepted, just as he accepted the fact that his feet were no longer on the ground. Volition was no longer his to command; he was at the mercy of the merciless, and as he moved across the bizarre, visceral landscape, his anxieties climbed like some heinous sunrise.

Then he saw the saltire crosses, and the figures tied to them. There were three in total, the blackened wooden roods slick with blood that wept from the splayed wrists and ankles of the people with bonds pulled so tightly upon the skin that it bulged and split as the thongs ate into the flesh. Like the roots of a tree circumnavigating rocky ground, the hands and feet were bent at right angles, where the bones had grown in the only direction they could.

To his horror, Ray could see the bodies hanging from the crosses shuddering as they tried to draw breath, their torsos covered in bloodied, shitty rags. The familiar frozen masks they wore were fixed to their heads, making it difficult for Ray to determine gender, but the hideous moans that came from beneath the frozen faces made plain the agony each endured.

Mere feet away from the crucified forms, Ray landed on the ground, tripping as his feet became tangled. He threw his arms forward to stay his fall, and where his palms met the scarlet grass, so too did pools of blood spread out beneath his hands. His knees felt the hideous warmth as it seeped through the material of his trousers, and at that moment he realised that this was perhaps the most vivid apparition he'd ever experienced.

He looked up at the figure directly above him, watching the crimson cataract as it oozed from the terrible wounds. A guttural cry came from beneath the mask and a hideous tearing sound came to him. His eyes widened as he saw the rags split open at the abdomen, bloody coils slopping out, spraying his face with their heat.

Ray staggered backwards, his own scream piercing the moment. Then the image was gone, and he was, once more, in the bathroom at Trust HQ.

But he wasn't alone.

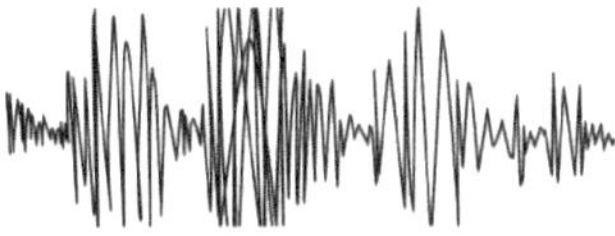

"You want to tell me what *that* was all about?" Mike asked, his mouth pulled straight by grim concern.

Ray was leaning against the bank of sink units, the porcelain putting a cool line in his lower back. When he'd yanked himself out of the vision, he'd been crawling around the washroom floor like a tired dog looking for a place to lie down. When he'd seen Mike staring down at him, he'd fought his way to his feet, despite the wooziness threatening to drag him back to the ground.

"I just felt a little dizzy, that's all," Ray said. His voice was watery and lacked enthusiasm.

"And the yelling? It's a wonder half the building isn't in here."

Ray's response was brisk. "I panicked."

He was impressed at how fast he was able to deliver such bullshit. Maybe he was getting used to the idea that he was losing his mind. Given where he worked, he figured there were worse places in which to yield to madness.

Mike put his hand into the pockets of his baggy trousers, his shoulders slumping. Ray couldn't gauge if the big man had bought his story or not, and at that moment found that he didn't really care.

All he could see was the terrible images of crucified, tortured people drowning in blood as he tried to figure out what the fuck it all meant.

"Maybe you should take some time off?" Mike suggested.

"Can't. I've got to present to the CGC in ten minutes. No getting out of it. Not without looking bad."

What you mean is without looking weak, his inner voice corrected him. *That's where the rot sets into a career in upper management, isn't it? When those calling the shots sense you're not up to the stresses that come with the job.*

"Damn it," Ray said under his breath.

Mike shook his head. "You can't present if you're sick, boss. Why can't Eloise do it?"

"It's not fair on her. She's had no prep time."

Ray turned to the wall of mirrors behind the sink units. His face was ashen and his eyes bloodshot. "Shit, I look like I've been on the piss."

Mike chuckled. "Well, there are worse ways to try and get through the day."

Hitting the faucet, Ray doused his face. The relief of the icy water was instant, shocking away the last vestiges of his vision.

"You sure you're okay, boss?"

Ray mopped his face with several paper towels from the wall dispenser. "Yeah, I'm good. Thanks."

He doubted Mike believed his response any more than he did.

CHAPTER SIXTEEN

DENISE headed into the delivery suite reception area, the buzz of activity around her immediately generating excitement. She loved her job. It defined her, and for as long as she could remember, midwifery had been her only sure goal in life.

She'd worked at Birmingham Women's Hospital for over ten years, during that time rising from shift leader to ward manager, and then to matron. Her guile and aptitude for organisational change and a caring, approachable demeanour proving to be a boon in career progression.

Taking on the Consultant Midwife title had been the turning point at a career crossroads; one pathway leading to Head of Midwifery and directorate level management, the other to senior clinical roles. Her heart had always been in midwifery practice, so the choice had been relatively easy, the consultancy role offering a balance between strategic and clinical influence. A perfect fit that she wore very, very well.

Her phone vibrated in her fleeced jacket. She looked down at the text message as soon as she dug the phone out of her pocket.

No earring, my love. Perhaps I should buy you some more? You can wear them and nothing else. Yum, yum. Peter x

While she deleted the message, she toyed with the idea of blocking his number, then, with a tut, decided otherwise.

No point in riling him, she thought. *No point in risking him coming to the house.* She supressed the quite fear that came with such a thought and crossed the reception area, forcing herself to concentrate on work.

With security pass in hand, she intended to access the doors leading into the belly of the building. The lanyard swung loosely about her neck when she heard her name ring out.

"Denise! Wait up!"

She turned to see Anita Robinson—the reception clerk—waving at her, a triad of silver bangles jangling as they slid down to her forearm. Anita was tall and slim with wild, white hair. She had a thin nose and huge glasses that reminded Denise of those worn by TV comic Harry Hill. When she wasn't behind the large, veneered reception counter, Anita could be found three paces beyond the Trust boundary having a cigarette, usually leaning up against the 'We Are a No Smoking Trust' sign.

Denise went up to the desk, where the receptionist smiled broadly.

"Got something for you," Anita said. She disappeared behind the counter and then came back, a large cardboard package in her hands. "Ooh, presents!"

Denise looked warily at the box. "I wasn't expecting anything."

"They're the best kind, right?"

Save for the postal information, the box was plain, and that was enough to tell Denise who it was from. Like the leather bracelets and gown she'd received earlier, the innocuous package spoke only of mystery, and her heart raced with fear.

But there was also a kernel of anger in her gut. Peter was fast becoming an irritant. She was going to have to be more direct, it seemed. Especially after his antics the previous morning.

Anita's eyes glinted expectantly. "Are you going to open it?"

"No point in getting a parcel if I'm not going to open it," Denise chuckled.

"No, I mean are you going to open it *now*?"

"No," Denise said. It came out slightly faster than she wanted it to, but she recovered quickly. "I'm heading straight into a meeting, so don't want to spoil the moment."

Anita appeared to buy it. "Well, you make sure you keep me in the loop. I have to enjoy presents by proxy these days. It gets me through the day."

"I'll let you know for sure," Denise said, lifting the box. It was very light, and she managed it with ease.

Before Anita could continue with her queries, a group of visitors arrived—en masse—demanding her attention. Denise used the distraction to move away.

By the time she'd got to her office and closed the door behind her, she had a suspicion that whatever was in the box was not going to be for common knowledge. It was a clandestine gift for a private encounter, and given her experiences with Peter over the past few months, Anita was the last person with whom Denise would share the contents.

She left the box unopened and beneath her desk. Ultimately, she would not open it until much later, and release the nightmare that was to come.

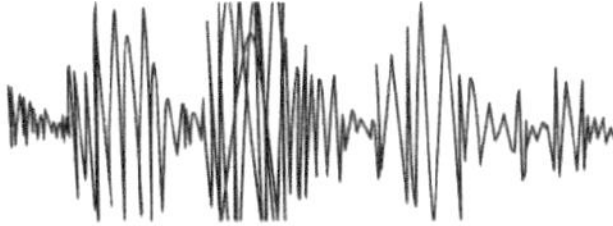

Mike sauntered over to Eloise's desk. His initial plan was to tell her about his concerns for Ray's well-being, but he thought better of it. This wasn't really his business, and if anyone should be telling Eloise about their boss, he figured it should *be* their boss.

As usual, he found her deep in thought, her eyes focused on the datasets on the screen. He watched her tapping a biro against her lower lip as she took in the facts and figures.

"You know the amount of bugs that accumulate on the average work biro?" he cautioned.

She smiled and turned to him. "Not as many as the average computer keyboard. Latest stats suggest you get more E. coli bacteria from a keypad than a toilet seat. Given the odds, I figure that puts you at greater risk than me."

He grinned. "Maybe. But the amount of shit I have to swallow here on a daily basis will probably render me immune."

She shook her head. "You're gross. But you know that, right?"

"Fact."

"And proud of it, too."

"You have to tout whatever wares you got."

"Well, there are worse things, I guess."

Mike noticed Eloise's eyes glance over his shoulder. For a second, he thought he could see her shoulders shiver.

Instinctively, he looked behind him and saw Brendan in the distance, emptying a waste paper bin. He turned back to her, puzzled.

"Are you okay?"

"What do you make of Brendan?"

"Not really thought about it. He's just kinda *there*, you know? In the background. Why?"

"Don't you think he's a bit—" she stalled, appearing to be having trouble finding the right word. "Creepy?" she said eventually.

Mike didn't hide his confusion. "In what way?"

"I don't know. In a *creepy* way."

Mike looked back at the domestic. "Is he giving you a hard time?"

"No. Not at all," she lied. "It's just me being stupid. Forget I said anything, okay?"

"Why don't I believe you?"

"Because most of the time you don't believe anyone?" she offered.

"That is pretty accurate. But are you sure nothing's wrong?"

"Haven't you got work to do?" she said with a giggle.

"Rumour has it," he said as he went back to his desk.

He sat down, his eyes going back to Brendan who was now heading down the stairs to the lower floor. The fact that Eloise hadn't responded to Mike's last question had not been lost on him, and now something had taken up residency in his stomach.

Anger. Seething and broiling fury.

And, in such instances, there was only one thing that could placate him. The feeling always left him with a great sense of loss, an intense empty sensation that fuelled resentment and fed the ire. He knew he would have to do something to quell it.

And soon.

CHAPTER SEVENTEEN

EVEN as Brendan lingered by the hedgerow, body standing back from the privet so that he could barely be seen by anyone walking towards him, he did not—would not—consider himself a stalker. There had been a time when he'd questioned such things; for instance, when he was younger, and he was trying to establish his place in the world.

He'd always been drawn to watching girls, revelling in the thrill of it. Over time he'd honed the art, becoming a chameleon, eyes keen and focused. He preferred small breasts; *any more than a handful is a waste,* his old man had been fond of saying, and Brendan lived by this edict.

Hugh Short, his bullish father, was a lover of women, but beyond the physicality of sex, he possessed little love *for* them. Hugh worked steel in a Dudley foundry until his retirement. It was hard, physical work, and he was shaped by its harsh caress. In contrast, Maeve—Brendan's mother—was a slight, feisty woman, just the right side of five feet tall, with long, black hair, and a temper to easily match that of her husband. She was long-suffering and tenacious, the recipient of countless affairs at the hands of her philandering spouse.

Despite the infidelity, Brendan's parents stayed together, and the reason why they were still married until their deaths (two years apart, with Hugh going first in 1981) was the fact that they loved each other on an intrinsic level. Yes, it was a strange and dysfunctional kind of love, but it had strength and thus endured, going deeper than most could claim.

Sex was always the best medicine in the family home; it cured all ailments, mended all disputes. A young Brendan would listen to his parents making up after their latest fight—paper-thin walls a mere membrane, barely muting lust and climax, keeping him awake and making him irritable when he was too young to recognise what his parents were actually doing.

As time went on, irritation and inconvenience morphed into curiosity as to why his parents moaned and gasped behind the wall. One day, he decided that he wanted to see what was going on. So, at nine years of age, he borrowed his father's hand drill and made a peephole in his bedroom wall, hiding it behind a Judas Priest poster. Singer Rob Halford and guitarist Glenn Tipton stood clad in leather and studs, concealing Brendan's little secret from his parents. In his parent's bedroom, the exit of the tell-tale peephole was hidden well in the heavily patterned wallpaper.

By the time Brendan was twelve years old he was an assured voyeur, peeping at his parent's nocturnal encounters whenever he got the chance. Watching others became a blueprint for his life—first through porn videos, then the Internet. But he found the medium sanitised and distant, no replacement for actually *being there*, watching as he had with his parents.

He moved on to strip clubs and brothels, hiring private booths where he could watch in comfort. Here he met Judith White, his partner of over ten years. They shared an interest in theatre, stage shows in particular. That she should prefer live performances to cinema came as no surprise to Brendan.

He'd watched Judith have sex with several men over a period of eight weeks before meeting her one afternoon in her local store. It had all been contrived, of course—Brendan lived over three miles away from the Spa supermarket where he'd *accidentally* bumped into her and knocked the basket of fruit she'd been carrying to the floor in full rom-com cliché.

All apologies, he helped her collect the basket, offering to pay for the contents. He'd convinced himself then—and he knew it for certain now—that there was a connection between them that would have occurred even without his clandestine fixation. For in the supermarket all those years ago, Brendan saw a sense of loneliness in Judith's eyes that mirrored his own.

He offered to buy her a drink by way of an apology for his 'clumsiness', and she had agreed. In a nearby pub, their conversation flowed without any awkwardness, and before long they were talking about the theatre. From that point on, their relationship began.

For the next few months, Brendan and Judith played a game. In this game, Judith pretended that she was going out to work in a local restaurant, and Brendan pretended to believe her. As far as they were both concerned, neither of them had cause nor inclination to reveal the reality of their fledgeling relationship. There was no sex in those early days, just a friendship that neither sought to progress.

Then one evening, after watching a damn good production of *Stagecoach*, Brendan gave Judith an 'out'. He confessed that he had a penchant for watching people have sex, and he'd paid for such experiences. It was all an act—he left out that he'd watched *her*, going as far as saying that it was a part of his life that he wished he could change. Even as he finished his story, he could see Judith start to relax. Within the next hour, she had disclosed her real job. Reluctantly at first, fearing the backlash, but when he reached over and squeezed her hand, she leaned her head into his shoulder and wept with relief. Later that same evening they had made love for the first time, and for Brendan, the act seemed discordant, his climax not matching the intensity his voyeuristic endeavours brought him. But it was enough to cement their relationship for the years ahead.

The only lie Brendan maintained was that he never admitted he'd watched her before they had met, the privacy afforded by the booths at her club helping the ruse. He did, however, ask if she ever did such things and, if that was the case, would she be prepared to have him observe her at work.

She was admittedly uncomfortable with the notion at first, but relented when she saw his need to fulfil this part of his personality. She told him how much she loved him because he accepted her for who she was, and from then until a few years ago, when her aged body gave in to a stroke, Brendan had watched his partner have sex with others and remained the happiest man in the world.

Things were different now. Judith was dead, but his urges were as alive and insistent as ever, albeit in desperate need of *focus*.

And in Ellie, he believed he'd found such a thing.

He watched her approach and thought about reaching into his pants and touching himself. At the last minute he ducked out of sight behind the hedge, his work colleague passing him by, oblivious to his presence.

He peered out, watching Eloise's taut buttocks sway in her skirt. She headed off towards the supermarket multi-storey car park across the busy A road, where her Fiat 125 was parked with agreement with store management. She disappeared into the building, the sliding glass doors giving her access. Once she was inside, Brendan decided to move.

He knew where Eloise would be headed; he'd memorised her routine to the letter. After work, she would head straight to the gym, and from there, showered and freshened up, she would head back home to curl up in front of the TV after a steak salad and a glass of wine.

Brendan was aware of Eloise's post-work routine because he'd been watching her for the best part of a week. The exhilaration of hiding in the shadows, a silent sentinel as she sat oblivious to his gaze from the blackness of her back garden, was incredible, but paled in comparison to what had happened when his fingers had touched hers earlier in the day.

He felt as though he needed more than the mere sight of her, needed to *connect* in some way. He wasn't sure what that meant, but he knew it would have to involve some kind of contact. Perhaps an item of clothing would suffice. Something *personal*.

It was as he considered the thought of stroking a pair of Eloise's thongs that a shadow appeared to his left, and a huge hand slapped down on his shoulder.

Panicked, Brendan looked up at the newcomer, surprised to see Mike's angry face staring at him.

"You and me need to have a little chat," the big man growled.

Brendan's tone was sour, and devoid of contrition. "About what?"

"For starters, you can tell me what the fuck you're up to?" Mike clarified as he tried to keep his temper in check. He was clearly failing miserably. As he spoke, he could feel his bottom lip trembling, and his carotid artery throbbed like a taut wire in his neck.

"I could ask you the same thing," Brendan replied. His voice was small, a squeak against a lion's roar. "I'm not used to being *physically assaulted* at work."

"You don't know what physical assault is," Mike said in a hoarse voice. "If you don't leave Eloise alone, I can certainly show you the real deal."

Brendan's eyes may have shown fear, but his mouth failed to catch on. His reply was fast and direct. "You saying Eloise put you up to this? What is this, are you her hired help or something?"

"Watch your mouth, Brendan. Or you'll be losing teeth."

"You'll be losing a lot more," Brendan said flatly. "And for nothing. It's not a crime to stand by a hedge these days. Or have I missed the police bulletin?"

"What? So you just *happened* to be lurking here, watching Eloise crossing the road?" Mike scoffed. "She's spooked by you, get it? You need to give her a wide berth from now on."

Brendan smirked. "Just listen to yourself. You get any more paranoid and you're likely to get sectioned. At least they won't have to drag you far. I don't care what she's told you or what you think. I haven't said or done anything to her." He paused. "Maybe tomorrow we could go and ask her what I'm supposed to have done?"

Mike blanched. "There's no need to do that."

Brendan smiled enough for Mike to want to knock him out.

"All *that* tells me is she doesn't know you're here. Maybe you saw this as a way to win her affections? A two-ton knight in brown, baggy trousers and all that."

Mike said nothing. His face was a mix of simmering anger and fear, but the latter emotion had the edge.

"I'd suggest you get the fuck out of my way, Mike. Or my next job won't be bleaching the CEO's toilet. It'll be letting Eloise know she's got a not-so-secret admirer. All you have to do is work out how she's likely to respond to that little news item. You're the analyst—what are the odds on that ending well for your working relationship?"

Brendan pushed by Mike, who made no attempt to stop him. The big man watched the domestic disappear behind the hedge, his thoughts staying with the last words Brendan had said.

No, the odds that this would destroy *any* relationship with Eloise were surefire. And just as certain were the odds of Brendan holding this knowledge over him going forward. The decision that he needed to do something about it came shortly afterwards.

People—good people—respond well to a grand gesture, the voice of his mother said in his head. *Lies and deceit are the enemies of friendship. If you are true to yourself then others will invest in you, trust you. And from trust, only good things can grow.*

Mike decided he needed the type of grand gesture his mother had spoken of in the past. He came up with a plan of action, and it involved drawing upon his innate skill to rectify a spiralling situation. He figured he could get the deed done over the next few nights, and then he may just undo any damage Brendan doled out on his relationship with Eloise. It also involved taking a risk, but he had to try.

He was moving again, following in Brendan's footsteps, and the smile was back on his face.

CHAPTER EIGHTEEN

"CAN we take a break?" Ray's eyes were becoming even more red-rimmed. "I need some time to think."

Cross nodded. "Interview paused at 13:55 for a comfort break." He hit the pause button on the recording device, the click loud in the oppressive atmosphere.

In front of him, Ray made no acknowledgement of his action. In fact, he appeared to be staring off into space, as though he was an arcade animatronic in need of a few pennies. The absence in his eyes made Cross feel oddly uncomfortable.

Without warning, Ray spoke. "Don't you ever need this?"

"What?" Cross asked, playing with his smartphone.

"Time to just, you know, *wink out?*"

Cross considered this for a few moments. "Maybe. When we've had a bad shout."

What Cross really meant was 'most certainly'. He'd seen some fucked up shit in his time, and that kind of stuff lingered—left you feeling dirty—and the last thing he wanted to do was to have it stain his family life. He'd heard too many tales, from too many cops, about how the terrible things people did to each other in the name of love, hate, and economics, could impact on the home life of a police officer. As a result, the divorce courts were littered with more casualties than a gangland hit.

To this end, Cross had a ritual: he'd head home, often refusing a visit to the pub that seemed to be his colleagues' antidote to a shit day. Under normal circumstances, his car journey took forty minutes, but as far as his wife and six-year-old daughter were concerned, it took an hour and fifteen. Cross would park up his car ten minutes from the house, turn off the engine, and hit the Bluetooth connection for his smartphone.

For the next thirty minutes, he would listen to *Rammstein*, the aggressive riff-heavy sounds of the German industrial metal band purging him of his frustrations and despair. He would sing along at the top of his voice, palms slapping against the steering wheel, feet pummelling the footwell, his mind attempting to bleach the dirt of the day from his spirit. By the time he'd completed his ritual, an innate peace would descend, the 'detective' parked for another day. He was just husband and father, heading home to be with his family.

He never questioned how it came to be, but as a process, it was effective—it *worked*, and that was all that mattered to him in the end. His wife wouldn't have to hear about the dreadful things he'd witnessed: sex workers battered to death by their drunken, shit-bag pimp boyfriends who hired them out like fucking power tools, kids abused and neglected by degenerate parents that needed a bullet to the brain rather than re-education, and the blood—so much blood—and pain, and loss. It was all a filthy cloak that his ritual helped him to discard, so he could be wholesome and good and kind, the very things that so many people he met during the course of his work would never truly understand.

Cross rubbed an itch at his brow. "You want some coffee? Tea, maybe?"

Ray shook his head. "No. Let's carry on."

"Sure," Cross said, activating the machine. "Interview with witness Raymond Tonks resumes at 14:00."

Ray began speaking again, and the detective sat opposite, longing to be back in his car listening to Rammstein.

CHAPTER NINETEEN

At breakfast, Ray flipped through his paperwork for a board meeting later that day, trying to find his place. The house was quiet, not even the radio playing forum. Denise had also left early, keen to beat the traffic hell that was the A38 Northbound into the city.

His thoughts were restless, which was not unusual when he'd had a vision; the kind of things he was exposed to when they happened wasn't really conducive to peace of mind. Furthermore, there was the issue of how he was coping with the latest bout. Firstly, he was no longer calling them *visions*; their abstract nature separated them from his traditional experiences. Instead, he was calling them *attacks*. It didn't really help in any realistic sense, but by rebranding the experience, it at least made him feel as though he could control some element of this phenomenon, as token as it was. And, in truth, he felt that the term more accurately described their effect on him, an assault on his senses at every level.

Another way of dealing with his attacks was to clarify if they were different. At one point, he'd convinced himself that he was witnessing events that just hadn't made the news or were yet to be discovered by police. For the first time since his teens, he actively scanned the news outlets—online and on TV—to see if there were any stories that were related to his attacks. He'd found nothing, but the thought that he should perhaps contact the police and explain what was happening was immediately discounted. Besides, what he was seeing this time around was so *fucked up*, it would be difficult to describe, let alone explain how he'd got to be a witness. He'd seen the treatment psychics received on a daily basis, and his old school fears of ridicule stamped out the idea as soon as the first shoots sprouted.

With a sigh, he tried to focus on the papers, on anything to get his mind out of the mire it was so damned keen to wade through.

He'd forced himself to read two paragraphs before the pages disappeared and he found himself in a world of his own creation.

Where the sky was alive with fire.

Lightning streaks sent pulsating veins through the black and bloated clouds, and the huge blasts of thunder seemed to make the very air vibrate. The rain came like a cataract, water pouring in fat drops, splattering the pavement, soaking him to his skin. Ray, however, felt nothing at all. Not the material of his clothes as it stuck to his skin, not the rainwater as it poured down his face in streams. He moved in slow motion, as though the weight of his waterlogged clothing was impeding all progress.

He was drawn to the sound that seemed to be impervious to the deafening din of the storm overhead. It was a thin, melodic sound—the sound of music. A note held, 'A minor' stretching out through the scene, the thunder punctuating the cadence. The landscape ahead was one of dark buildings, chunky behemoths lurking in the storm. When the lightning touched the sky, the edges of these oblong structures shimmered.

Ray went towards the nearest building, his feet sloshing through accumulated puddles on the tarmac. He approached a door, made small by the oppressive shadow of the wall towering over it. Before his fingers touched the metal of the handle, the door opened of its own accord, and he stepped through. Inside the music was loud, his ears protesting, his eyes watering, and he saw the bizarre image at the centre of the hangar. It was a sizzling streak of lightning and a blackened body, but the shaft of light did not wain, nor did the blackened, sizzling image fall to the ground. The body merely jittered on the spot, one leg poised in mid-step, the arms in midswing. There were no features, the clothes gone, the skin also seared and crisped to char-grill black.

Without warning, more shapes appeared from behind the

burning image. He looked as the thing with the zippered eyes and a bloodied woman clad in rags with the gold and blue face emerged. Under the sputtering light, the two images seemed to morph into one, becoming a twisted shape comprised of stitches, frozen faces and blood. Again, the snakes of gore slithered from the woman's abdomen, and this time they cooked under the heat of the lightning bolt.

Ray reeled away from the sight of it all, his mouth open and gagging at the stench that hit him as the meat began to roast.

When the image left him, he was already unloading his tea and toast into his lap, the copy of his quarterly board report lost forever.

Denise leaned against the body of her car. From the hem of trees that demarcated the makeshift car park boundary, the undulating landscape of the Lickey Hills rose before her. To her right, a muddy dirt path led to the visitor's centre, an oblong wooden chalet turned murky grey by a mist of fine rain.

She turned the collar of her overcoat against the brisk wind coming in from the west, yet its touch still found her neck, and she shivered. She'd told Ray she had to be in work early, but she'd actually taken the day off.

Like her husband, she was pensive; the events of recent times appeared to be escalating. She'd sought out ways to break with routine and the trappings of control, and for a while, she had welcomed and revelled in them. But now such things were a leash she needed to sever. She had to make Peter understand that all this had to end, and it had to end now.

In the boot of her car, the last gift remained unopened. For some reason, she thought that opening the box and revealing its contents would start a process she truly wanted to end before it began. The regret was growing, and joining it was remorse that she feared would become rampant. What happened should *never* have happened; the risks, simply not worth it.

This was made evident by all the sneaking around she'd been doing since starting this madness in the first place. On the day she'd got the last gift, she'd snuck out of work later than usual. Not because she was busy, but to avoid Anita and her prying questions about the contents of her mysterious package.

"Goddamn it," she whispered to the wind, and went to the boot, pulling out the damning carton.

She carried it with her and climbed into the car. A thick strip of brown tape sealed the box. As much as she wanted to just take all of the items and throw them into a skip, her inquisitiveness got the better of her. Now, as the rain put streaks on the windshield, Denise dragged the box towards her. She adjusted her seat, pushing it back to make room on her lap. She used her front door key to saw open the tape and pulled the cardboard leaves open. Inside was a mound of white packing material—polystyrene tubes—some of which spilt out onto her uniform. She rummaged in the box, and the first thing she found was the card.

It was in an envelope, and on the surface was her name written in Peter's usual handwriting.

Guilt and irritation came to her at the same time, and the thought crossed her mind that she was starting to deeply dislike this man. Inside the envelope was a black card with a white pathos mask upon it. In there, she found a note that simply said:

This is your third gift.

Ring me.

She threw the card on the seat and delved inside the box, her hands finding the edges of something cool and firm. She took hold and lifted the item from the sea of packing foam.

"What the fuck is this?" she whispered.

CHAPTER TWENTY

In the boardroom, Ray prepped his notes. The sheets of paper shivered in his grasp, betraying his anxiety. He found his current state of mind a frustration. Presentations to Trust Board were nerve-wracking enough without the addition of bizarre, terrifying images that seemed determined to drop into his head without the usual aura.

For now, he was determined to park those thoughts. His focus had to be on the next half hour, where a ten-slide PowerPoint presentation would inform the organisation's executive team of the Quality Account goals for mitigating risk over the next three-year cycle.

The room was oblong, the walls daubed in clinical blue. There was a table at the centre of the room made of several smaller desks. packed together to form an uneven wooden rectangle with yellow fascia. The executive team were sitting around the table, laptops and tablets before them, lids flipped, screens open, pumping out information. Ray suspected that most of the ten people would be more interested in their email streams than anything that came out of his mouth in the next thirty minutes. And yet, the people called in to present would all be wishing this shit could be done via the Teams platform, safely distanced from the quizzed looks, the bored or contemptuous faces. All eyes would no doubt pull in his direction when it came to the last slide—the *important* slide. The one that made recommendations as to how anything broken should be fixed. This was where the potential to spend or save money came from, and the 'bottom line' was king in the NHS' cash-strapped coffers.

Dean Travis, the CEO, was sitting directly opposite, his large frame the product of business schmooze and good living. At that moment, Travis was punching on the keys of his laptop, his pale eyes stern, calculating. Beside him sat Debbie Colman, the Deputy CEO and Director of Operations. She was a small woman with a blonde bob, and a face made smooth by Botox. Her brown eyes were sink-holes beneath heavy mascara.

"When you're ready, Ray," said Debbie, voice firm.

He acknowledged her with a nod.

To his right, a small lectern played host to a laptop, its black carcass hooked up to an interactive whiteboard, where the introductory slide was splashed upon the screen behind him. Ray hit the ENTER key and began his presentation.

As usual, the nerves left him as soon as he began to speak. His confidence came from knowing his job and knowing it well. In a room such as this, it didn't pay to be any different. In rooms like these, careers were made or destroyed. Maybe not immediately—that wasn't how things worked in the NHS. Instead, the demise would be an insidious, lingering process, the way a patient succumbs to a vile, terminal illness.

Ray felt himself detach, his extant knowledge propelling his presentation seamlessly forward, the executive team (or at least those who were listening) nodding in all the right places. He realised in that moment that there were to be no surprises for him, no curveballs that he'd have to duck or counter. He slipped into his groove, enjoying the minutes as they passed by.

His mother had once told him that pride often came before a fall. He'd laughed her pessimism off so many times in the past, he'd lost count. The phrase was a testament to the traditionally British aversion to arrogance.

But today, Ray was to find out that his mother's words were going to slam home like twin torpedoes into the belly of a warship.

And the results were to be as equally devastating.

The first hint that things were not quite as they seemed came when the CEO started to laugh. It began as a barely perceptible giggle, and then rose to a series of staccato titters behind his hairy hands.

Ray pressed on for a few more sentences, his plan being to plough through the awkwardness and address any issues Travis had with the contents of his presentation once he'd concluded his spiel. This plan was derailed in the few seconds that followed when the CEO's titters became loud barking laughter, hands failing to mute the sound.

No longer able to ignore the guffaws, Ray's eyes locked on Travis. As soon as he saw the CEO, Ray took a step backwards, bumping into the lectern and sending the laptop crashing to the floor.

Dean Travis sat with his head slightly tilted backwards, his eyes so wide they looked like that of an outlandish cartoon character caught in surprise. His skin appeared waxen, and his mouth seemed on loan from a woman with sensual lips. As he laughed, Travis's mouth oozed thick, white fluid that traversed his chin like the most bizarre Muller Yoghurt commercial ever. Still the guffaws came, this time thick with fluid, gaining volume as the other executives joined in.

Ray's eyes went to them in turn: all the board members were sat there, staring blankly, lips voluptuously female no matter the person, and the foul skein slopped down onto their suits. Their limbs were rigid, stretched out in front of them, palms flat as though they had been nailed to the table, and Ray could see stitched seams on each finger, as though Dr Frankenstein had tried his hand at organisational change management.

"Who the hell are you people?" Ray screamed. His terror was now festering, turning to rage in order to protect him from these hideous demons. In his mind, he feared the apparitions were exactly that—demons sent from Hell. And that somehow, his ability had become the conduit through which they were able to crawl.

At his cry, Travis stood. It was an ungainly sight. The CEO appeared unsteady, as though he was trying to walk on feet that were not his, and Ray had visions of Mary Shelly's maverick physician sewing dead limbs together in a lightning storm, not quite getting the stitching right.

Ray pushed himself backwards, but there was nowhere else to go. The wall barred his exit, and to his horror, the other board members were now climbing to their hideous feet, the room filled with squeaks and hisses.

Travis lumbered towards him, and Ray wished that he could get his own legs to move while trying to ignore the irony that out of every limb in the room, his were the only ones that *should* be working.

He saw Travis reach for him, goo spraying from his mouth as he coughed and gurgled, all sounds of laughter now gone. Splayed fingers creaked as they sought out Ray's face, and the hideous stench of fish and silicone made his eyes water.

Ray slapped away the hands. "Get the fuck away from me!"

A sudden, searing pain caught him in the temple and Ray felt his legs give out, the wall supporting him enough that he could slide to his backside. He felt distant and unconnected, a sense of relief passing through him, offering him some respite from the pain and horror. There was a resignation there too, an acceptance that if he never woke up again it would be okay, it would *all be okay*.

Hands were grabbing at him, and he waited to be torn apart, his innards uncoiled and strewn about the boardroom just like the images he'd seen on the saltire crosses. Maybe the portents were for him, leading him to this moment when Hell came to earth and claimed him for its own.

Discordant voices came next, urgent and etched with concern, and he weakly shook his head as though trying to be free of them.

"Okay, you can kill me, see if I care," he moaned. "God damn you all."

"Ray?" It was Travis's voice, and it was no longer coated with ooze. "Ray, can you hear me?"

Opening his eyes, Ray took a moment to take in the image. The demons were no longer there. They had been replaced instead by a Trust Board who looked down at him with expressions that demonstrated only concern and sorrow.

Even though he saw no malice or contempt, the faces of the ten people staring at him left Ray pining for the demons to return.

CHAPTER TWENTY-ONE

"Do you believe in God, Malcolm?"

"Does this have relevance to your testimony, Ray?"

Cross watched Ray shrug his shoulders. "Does it matter if it doesn't? You're 'paid by the hour', if I remember it right."

The detective smiled. "You got me."

"So, *do* you? Believe in God?"

"I believe in what religion represents."

"That's not what I asked."

"If you're talking mystical beings and Angels with trumpets, then no, I don't."

"But you do believe in *something*?"

"Like I said, I believe in what religion *represents*. Morality—being good to your fellow man. Our laws are defined by such things."

"Is that why you became a police officer?"

Malcolm thought this through. "Maybe."

"Are you a crusader, detective?"

This made Malcolm chuckle. "Fighting the good fight? Not quite in those terms, but I think the good should out-trump the bad. Or at least have a little help in making that happen."

Ray leaned forward, his forearms sliding on the table. "But what's good and bad ultimately depends on *individual* perspective, right? What *I* think is right, you may not."

"And that's where the law comes in to arbitrate, Ray," Malcolm ceded.

"So, it's the decisions of *people* that ultimately determines what is right or wrong. Have we not in ourselves become God, I wonder?"

Malcolm looked at Ray and saw only mischief in his eyes.

"Shall we continue?" the detective asked. His voice was firm, making it clear that this wasn't up for negotiation, nor was the interview a forum for ridicule.

The condescending snicker from his interviewee told Cross the jury was still out.

CHAPTER TWENTY-TWO

"Want to tell me what happened?"

Ray sat in Travis's office, where family photographs and NHS Improvement wall charts tried to bring colour to the insipid, beige environment. He'd been brought here shortly after his episode in the boardroom had passed. Fear and confusion had given way to embarrassment and vulnerability. But if any of the executives had sought to capitalise on such aspects, they did not show it. Travis certainly didn't as he poured out two coffees from the small espresso machine in the corner of his office.

"I'm not sure," Ray said as Travis handed him the coffee before sitting down on a chair opposite.

"This ever happened before?" Travis asked. His persona was matter of fact. Ray knew he had a background in emergency nursing, and guessed the CEO was going through the basics of an ED triage assessment.

"No. It's never happened before."

"You sure?"

Ray took a sip of his coffee. It was strong and bitter, but a good ruse to collect his thoughts. "Maybe once, a while ago. I got checked out, MRI and CT scans. They found nothing untoward."

"Interesting."

What was 'interesting' to Ray was that he'd never felt the need to extend the lies he perpetuated with his wife to the workplace. He figured that once you started spreading the untruths too thinly, the gaps would start to show. Despite this, as Travis eyed him with a nondescript expression, Ray found himself wishing he had something else in reserve to throw the CEO off the scent.

"So, what now?" Ray asked.

"*Now* I'd suggest heading over to ED and getting checked out. You got someone to drive you?"

Ray thought this over. Eloise came to mind almost immediately. "Yes. Perhaps we can go over the presentation before—"

Travis held up a hand. "Stop right there, Ray. I'm CEO of a mental health trust. One of my team members has just collapsed. What kind of a leader would I be if we talked shop before making sure you've got the all-clear from the medics?"

Ray nodded. "Yeah. Okay. Thank you."

"Just get yourself well," Travis said with a brief smile. Ray recognised the conflict in a man more comfortable with the governance machine, rather than the purpose it served. It made the gesture all the more potent.

"One more thing," Travis said as Ray stood on unsteady legs.

"Yes?"

"Time to start being more honest with people about your health."

Ray acknowledged him with a bob of his head and left the office. Once outside, he took in a deep breath and recalled the CEO's voice as he'd spoken the final words of their meeting. The tone had been firm, no-nonsense.

The unmistakable hallmarks of a first—and final—warning.

Brendan headed to his car, parked up in a side street. Over the past few days, he'd had time to think about his confrontation with Mike. He'd concluded that the run-in had been a strange affair. What should have been anxiety-provoking had left him feeling exhilarated beyond measure.

Despite these uncertainties, one thing was becoming clear: there was something building inside him, a dizzying sense of power that had started with the tentative touching of Eloise, and had been given greater impetus when he'd put Mike in his place. Times were changing—*he* was changing.

He'd taken to trying to understand why his focus had shifted to actually yearning for some form of physical contact after years of needing only to watch. Ultimately, he came to the decision that it had something to do with being alone now that his partner of long standing was no longer there with him. It made enough sense for him not to pursue it further—it was a can of dark emotions that he did not wish to prise open.

This was a new dawn, and he intended to embrace it without reservation. The ideal would be underwear, of course, something that had graced the most intimate areas of Eloise's anatomy. At some point he was going to have to engineer a way of obtaining some.

Perhaps it was this reason he'd been seen standing in Eloise's garden the other night. A subconscious shift in his needs. Maybe somewhere along the line, his intentions had moved from voyeur to staking out a home in order to assess how to procure personal items for later enjoyment?

Regardless, the act had been incredibly exciting, the danger almost bringing him to orgasm there and then. But he'd reined himself in, since he didn't want to become reckless to the point of actually being caught out. The last thing he wanted was the police involved.

He'd managed to avoid Mike during his shift, altering his schedule so that he cleared away the analyst's desk when he was at lunch rather than later in the afternoon, where he'd be sure to run into him. It also meant that he missed Eloise, but for now, that was a small price to pay.

He climbed into his old Ford Fiesta and prepped to head out to Eloise's gym, where he intended to wait patiently for her to emerge. As he got behind the wheel, his mind turned over images of Eloise naked, exposing her small breasts, her nipples tight and rubbing against his eager palm, white panties inviting, beckoning. His erection rubbed painfully against the restriction of his underwear, and he used this to rationalise setting it free.

But it was to be his right hand that gave it true release.

An intense light pours onto a large table. The wood is old and warped, partly by age, partly by the years of exposure to the materials that had seeped into its knotted, gnarled surface.

The legs are thick and bowed, and there are several deep scars where the timber has split. The wood is a deep umber, but made pale by the halogens high overhead. There are six of them, their heat countered by the air conditioning unit bolted to one of the cellar walls. Workbenches and low shelving units butt up against the remaining walls, the red bricks dusty with cobwebs.

There are tools, too. Thin blades and wide spatulas, fat needles and glue, and many spools of thick thread, all with one purpose: to put things together. It takes love and care and great, great skill to make the pieces on the table fit. Disparate and delicate—this is where things would be brought to life.

Where things were born.

Laid out on the table, under the lights and cooled by the air conditioning unit, are the body parts. Heads, torsos and limbs, they are placed in order, arms and legs at right angles to the edges of the table. The heads lined up in a row, the eye sockets dark and vacant pits. There are eyes, but they're stowed in jars on the shelving units, each pupil glittering like buttons under the spotlights.

The figure hunched over the table is sitting on a high stool with a leather seat. Big hands working a needle through tough, stubborn material. On occasion, the process stops as a large impatient sigh fills the cellar. Then, the sewing continues. And all the time, through pursed, dry lips, the figure sends out the high-pitched tune that almost resembles 'Whistle While You Work'.

CHAPTER TWENTY-THREE

Looking down at her mobile phone, Denise plucked up the courage to dial the number she'd just pulled up on the screen. Her reticence was tempered by the ever prevalent anger bubbling away in her psyche.

The call was answered after only three rings.

Peter's voice was hushed, breathless. "Hello, my love. I've been thinking of you."

"You're not getting the message, are you, Peter? Let me spell it out for you—this is over. Do you understand? It's finished. And in truth, it never should have started."

Peter chuckled. "But it *did* start, and we agreed on the rules of the game from the very beginning."

"And that's all it was. A game. And now it's over. Time to go back to real life. Before we hurt people."

"Real life?" Peter's tone was flat, sour. "*This* is real life, my love."

"For you, maybe. But not for me. I'm not going to tell you again. Leave me alone."

Peter interjected softly. "I'm sending you a photo. It may change your mind."

There was a pause, and her phone alerted her to an incoming image.

"You got it?"

"Yes," she whispered. There was coldness in her stomach as reality bled into the moment.

The lost earring sat there, on Peter's bare thigh. The diamond gave off starbursts.

"You told me you didn't have it."

"I lied."

"Why?"

"Because it's what we do, isn't it, my love? We lie so that we can have our special moments together."

She closed her eyes, her response terse. "What do you want, Peter?"

"You *know* what I want. It's what you want too."

"No. No, I do *not*."

Peter sighed. "See what I mean, my love? Lies, lies, lies. Now, you will do what I ask. Or the next place this image will go is to your husband's inbox. Maybe I can send the pictures I took of you when you climaxed so hard you wept?"

Incredulity laced her voice. "You took *photographs*?"

His reply was smug. "I did. I'm looking at one now. It's making me hard."

"You fucker." But the retort sounded hollow, crestfallen.

Silence. Then, "Those photos were my very own little secret. But I'm more than happy to share. So, my love, do you want me to do that? Do you want me to share them with good old Ray?"

Denise's voice was soft with fear. "No. Of course not."

"Then you will make sure you come to me. The place I have in Bromsgrove. Tonight. Are we clear?"

She shook her head even though he wasn't there to see it. "I can't, I—"

"Yes, you can," he said firmly. "And you *will*. Don't make me wait. Or you will be *punished*."

A shudder went through her as she took a breath to quell her thumping heart. She closed her eyes and welcomed the blackness.

"Okay. I'll be there at eight."

"Seven. Not a moment later."

The phone clicked off, leaving Denise staring at the earring on the screen and wondering where it had all gone so, so wrong.

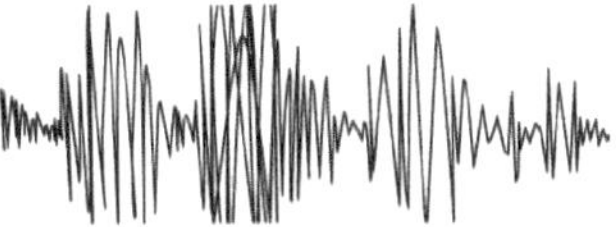

"You'll give me some notice if you start to feel iffy again, right?"

Eloise gave Ray a cursory glance as she nosed forward in the traffic. Her face had adopted a worried frown ever since Ray had asked her to take him to the hospital, even after he'd given her multiple assurances that he was okay.

He understood her concerns, of course. And he was just as unsure of whether his platitudes were accurate as his reluctant ride was.

"Honestly, I'm fine, Ellie."

A car horn beeped with impatience, reminding Eloise she needed to concentrate on getting them across the city to the ED in one piece. They sat in relative silence for the rest of the journey, Ray taking the time to attempt to contact Denise, and pondering on the terrible change in the presentation of his attacks.

Not since he was that same small boy, sitting in his hospital bed, did he feel so out-of-control, so confounded by what was happening. Once more, his mind flitted to the prospect of neurological damage. Foresight wasn't exactly a category in medical diagnostic manuals such as the ISCD or the American DSM-5, after all. There were no facts relating to how it could be treated, *if* it could be treated, and what the long-term effects were for anyone with it.

For all Ray knew, his brain was rebelling against the ongoing psychic assault, and deep down, he dreaded the worst. He feared that the vile episodes of recent times were some form of psychosis. On one level, he prayed the creatures he saw could not possibly be real. But there was no denying his ability to see bad things before they happened. So, if he could accept that as a premise, then it was impossible to deny that, somewhere in the world, these things existed and were running amok.

And this, perhaps, disturbed him more than the attacks themselves.

"We're here, Ray." Eloise broke into his reverie, and he was thankful for it. "I'll drop you at the entrance and go and find some parking."

He tentatively shook his head. "No need. I'll get hold of Denise. She can come and get me later."

Doubt returned to Eloise's face. "I'm not sure that's a good idea."

He sighed. "Ellie, I'm okay. Really. And you need to get yourself back to work. Mike can't be trusted to stay off *Elder Scrolls* unless you're breathing down his neck. Go, I'll let you know how it goes."

"Promise?"

"Yes. And thanks for the lift."

Before Eloise could protest further, Ray climbed from the car and closed the door behind him. He gave her a quick wave and headed off, disappearing through the glass doors without looking back.

IN the triage reception area, Ray leaned back in his seat and took several deep breaths. He hated hospitals, a paradox given his line of work—although he suspected its roots lay in that fateful day when he'd head-butted a rock. In many ways, his discomfort merely reinforced the historic divide commonplace in mental health and general medicine. Such things were never openly discussed; the professional rivalry was covert, a kind of therapeutic Cold War without end. Psychiatry was historically considered a charlatan practice, serving only to perpetuate the profession. Yet as a doctrine, madness served to elicit the mandates of social convention; the tolerance of rights and wrongs of current societal morality given form by asylums and institutions of the 19th century. When it came to funding, psychiatry was considered the poor relation to general medicine.

In nursing, the unspoken divide manifested in professional ambiguity and ignorance between specialities, a *never-the-twain* attitude between mental health nurses and their general counterparts. Ray watched two nurses, one male, one female—both in theatre scrubs— moving with determination through the area. Part of him envied the place society gave them in the world. People *wanted* to come here when they were ill. It was the first place they needed to be, a symbiotic relationship.

Such was not always the case in mental health, he'd found. The stigma associated with madness meant that those who suffered with mental illness tended to avoid talking about it until things were so far down the road, the only turn-off left open led to the car park of a psychiatric unit.

Detention under the Mental Health Act (MHA) was on the increase, highlighting just how reluctant people were to admission. And when forcibly detained in hospital under the State, people were labelled 'service users' or 'clients', pseudo-proponents of a system in which they really wanted no part.

Ray had spent so much of his clinical time enforcing the detention element of the MHA that the process of caring felt sullied, at least for him. Nurses had always been considered the statutory arm of enforcing The Act. 'Social Control', the philosophers and sociologists called it. In reality, it meant being stuck between a rock and a hard place, making mental health nursing an unenviably thankless job.

He felt bad about coming to such conclusions. His cynicism was not deeply ingrained, despite his issues and lived experience. He certainly hoped he'd never let such negativity show during his clinical years, especially to those to whom he delivered care. Getting out—using his experience to support staff at grass roots—was the only way he could rationalise leaving clinical practice. It felt right back then. It certainly did now.

A shadow fell upon him, and he looked up to see a figure in surgical scrubs. Ray began to speak, to impart he reason for being there, when his lips froze in horror.

The figure had no face.

CHAPTER TWENTY-FOUR

Brendan cursed so loudly, a young couple passing by his car looked at him before folding over with laughter and hurrying off. He watched them go as contempt raged in his eyes.

He was sitting in the car park of Eloise's gym, and her Fiat was nowhere to be seen. She *may have* gone home first, she *may have* caught the train in, and there were many 'may haves' and no *certainty* because of his own base need to jerk off instead of following her as he'd planned.

All of this was a new dynamic that he was still *coming to grips with*—in more ways than one, if he took the impromptu masturbation episode into consideration. His climax in the car had been beyond intense, but it had cost him time, and he'd been hampered by traffic all the way to the gym. Now he was going to have to pay the price.

He lingered at the site for another ten minutes, but deep inside he knew that his impulsivity had cost him. With an enraged hiss, he decided it was not meant to be and started the car. He hit the CD player and headed home, his head filled with the surging strings and horns of Wagner's *Tannhauser Overture*. The music soothed him, and as he pulled into the stream of traffic, humming a few bars, his mind was already pondering the cries Eloise made when she came.

As Eloise walked from the ED to her car, she thought about how strange the events of the past week had been. There was an off-kilter feel to life at that moment, a lack of equilibrium that made her unsettled.

The dream she'd had about her father's funeral still weighed heavy, and the nagging feeling that perhaps the figure in the garden had not been a figment of her imagination after all was starting to become very real.

Open discussion about Brendan had her questioning her own mind. She sensed something in the wily domestic, something predatory. The thought of this did not, however, make her feel vulnerable or frightened.

It made her angry.

Her mind was able to tap into something she had lost for quite a while. A place in her psyche where there was no sense of danger, where only a fierce determination to keep her life stable lurked. The seeds had been sown when she was young, of course. A four-year-old child with a drug-dependent mother could not completely walk away free from such a past. It was ever a shadow, and only in the dark times in her life did it resurface.

She climbed into her Fiat and concluded she would talk to Brendan directly about how he was making her feel. Her mother always told her that the true nature of a person could be seen in their eyes. Eloise wanted to look into Brendan's as she expressed her true feelings about his behaviour and establish if she was imagining things about him or not. Only then would she be able to decide on what she was prepared to do about it.

She returned back to the office and made a few phone calls. It was time to get a little balance back in her life.

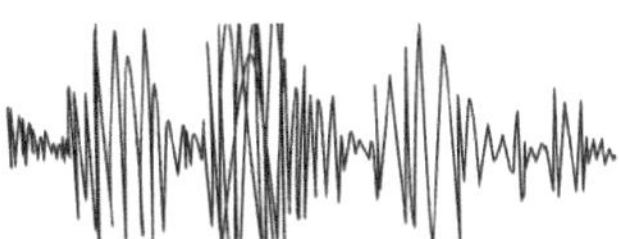

Ray squirmed in his seat as the ghastly image of the faceless nurse came closer. The scrubs bulged across its torso, and a sudden loud cracking sound ripped through the air. The material on either side of its sternum was speared by several bloodied prongs, which erupted from beneath. To Ray's revulsion, he realised that the ribcage had exploded outwards like the blooming petals of some gruesome flower.

The face continued to waver, making it unrecognisable when he dared look upon it. Behind the dreadful image, the ED had ceased to be, replaced instead by a great stairway made of red bricks and slabs, and lined with black, iron railings. This staircase led to a stone archway where, at the apex, twin gargoyles mated, their scaled skin glistening, claws tearing at each other's flesh as they writhed in ecstasy.

Twin doors of solid oak held firm in the arch, yet they shuddered under the blows of something unseen. After several loud thuds, these great doors bowed inwards before splitting asunder in a cloud of dust and splintering wood.

As the doors blasted inwards, Ray could see inside the building. There he recognised the crosses, the people impaled there crying and moaning, and the terrible wounds that were being inflicted on them by shadowy, stitched figures. There was blood and screams and the crack of whips, the grinding of blade against bone.

With incredible effort, he pulled his eyes away from it all, drawn now to the malformed nurse who suddenly had a face, a face that was screaming in agony.

It was *Denise*.

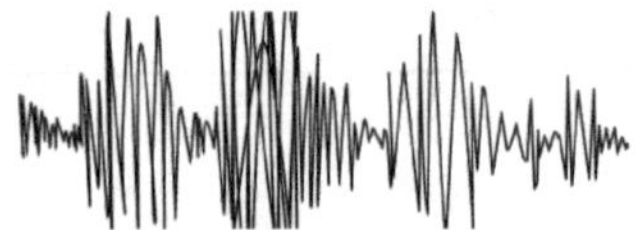

Mike tried to blink away the tiredness. His eyeballs felt as though they had been rolled in sand.

It was the morning after a very long night, but he hoped that his efforts would be appreciated. He knew he had to do something to soften the harshness of Brendan's inference, that he'd tell Eloise of Mike's feelings for her. Yes, it may have been an empty threat—a pre-emptive strike to warn him off—but Mike recognised he'd need some kind of contingency to mute the blow.

At first, he considered just telling Eloise outright, taking the chance despite the inevitability of it all. Then he thought through the consequences, and that was when his irritation got the better of him.

It was a trait his parents had often put down to his repressed feelings of being bullied for such a long time. For a few years they tolerated his tantrums, the throwing of items—some expensive, some sentimental, but all with explosive venom. They hoped it would merely be a phase, but for a while, it didn't seem to show any sign of reprieve.

During one particular outburst, Mike had broken something quite dear to his mother. It was a Victorian doll, its porcelain face beautifully painted, the clothes, exquisite. The doll had been a wedding gift to his mother from Mike's grandmother. It was pretty much irreplaceable.

His mother was heartbroken, and the sight of her clutching the shattered shell, as though cradling a dead infant, had emotionally crushed him. His guilt carved its name into his psyche, and he turned the anger on himself, quietly loathing his ability to destroy something so precious as his mother's love.

In that one action, he had become the very thing he reviled in life: a destructive force that sought to hurt through wanton acts of destruction. Yet this was immediately fused with the desire to be creative, and so his need to assemble things from acts of devastation was born. His craft could only create works of love and devotion.

It was the right thing to do. Not everyone would understand, of course. That was why he kept his *hobby* secret.

But when he thought of Brendan and the ire that came with it, Mike's instinct to build—to create—took over in the only way it knew how.

Last night he had done exactly that, building something quite beautiful that he intended to present to Eloise in the hope she would understand how he felt; enough to at least forgive anything a vengeful Brendan may say. It had worked before, after all. How could it not work now, at a time of great need?

Even in his weariness, he was excited at the prospect. He couldn't wait to see Eloise's face when he showed her what he'd made for her.

CHAPTER TWENTY-FIVE

R̲ay staggered from the ED department, his head crammed with confusing thoughts and images, all of them blurring into one swirling mess, assaulting his psyche, burning through his brain with the deadly efficiency of a wildfire. His vision fogged and his journey from the reception area to the exit was haphazard. The halogen streetlights beyond the large plate windows spangled under his gaze, making him moan with pain.

He heard distant questions from the nurses he passed, their voices etched with concern, but he waved them away, fighting to keep the contents of his stomach in check.

Outside, he allowed the cool air to wash over him, and after a few seconds, his vision cleared, leaving only a dull ache behind his eyes. Instinctively, he pulled his phone from his pocket and looked down at the last text he received from his wife. He wasn't surprised by her curt response, nor could he blame her—as far as she was concerned, he was neglectful of his medication regimen, and visits to ED were an inevitable outcome. Hence, he was now a victim of his own bullshit.

He tried to call, but her phone went straight to voicemail, and he left a panicked message asking her to get back in touch. He looked about him, eager to find a way to get back home.

Ahead, there was an ambulance bay where several front-line paramedic vans were parked up, waiting to offload. Behind the bay was another flat area of tarmac, and he could have shouted for joy when he saw that there were three cars lined up in the taxi rank. He headed over to the lead vehicle, where a middle-aged Asian guy in a Sikh turban sat reading something on his phone.

"Are you waiting for anyone?" Ray said.

"No, I'm good," the taxi driver replied brightly. "Where to?"

Ray went to the back of the car and climbed in. Once he'd shut the door he scanned the screen on his cell phone.

"Where are we going, mate? This is a taxi, it takes people places. But I still need to know where, okay?" Dimming the screen, Ray placed his phone in a cradle on his lap. The driver gunned the engine, and the headlights turned the 'Taxis Only' sign ahead to a shimmering yellow.

Ray gave his home address. "If you could, you know, get me there quickly, there might be a healthy tip for you?'

The taxi driver looked back at him through the rearview mirror. "Yeah, that'll come in handy when I have to pay the speeding fine."

Ray nodded in understanding. The car pulled off and he was left to stare out of the windows, not seeing anything other than his own despairing reflection looking back at him.

As soon as she pulled the car over at Peter's rendezvous point, Denise saw that she had five missed calls from Ray on her cell phone. They pinged through as soon as she activated her phone, which had been turned off as she drove out of the city and back to Bromsgrove.

There were also text messages. She looked down at them, eyes sad, giving a small nod as she scrolled through.

Ray: I had a blackout. Don't worry, I'm at ED. Can you come and give me a lift?

"Damn it, Ray," she muttered. "When are you going to learn to take your pills on time?"

The phone vibrated in her hand, startling her. She looked down at the 'incoming call' message, expecting to see her husband's caller ID, but instead it was their faux 'Carla' number scrawled across the screen.

She answered quickly. "Peter?"

"I can see you. Why have you not come in?"

"My husband is sick. He needs me to go and get him from hospital."

There was a drawn-out pause. The seconds were beat out by the pulse in her temple.

She ended the silence. "Are you still there?"

"Yes."

"Did you hear what I said?"

"It seems you did not hear *me*," he said slowly. "I set out the rules. Was I not clear?"

Denise was chewing the inside of her cheek with frustration. She composed herself before she answered.

"My husband needs me."

"*I* need you. I need you to play the game. I need to hear you lose control like you always do. Are you saying you no longer wish to play?"

"You already know the answer to that. I've said it's ov—"

"If you deny me then the game is forfeit, and you'll bear the consequences. As will your husband when he finds out what *naughty Denise* has been up to in his absence. Is that what you want? Is that how you wish to be *punished* today?"

Denise shook her head as though Peter was there to see it. "No, I don't want that," she whispered.

"Then get out of the fucking car and get up here," Peter said in a voice that was so calm he may have been ordering pizza.

The phone went dead, and she looked down at the inert rectangle of glass and plastic in her trembling palm.

"You little shit!" she said with venom. She had no choice, yet she still went through the motions of weighing out the options, hoping that calm rationality would help justify her forthcoming actions.

This wasn't the first time Ray had blacked out and ended up at the hospital. It wouldn't be the last. Recovery was standard, without any residual effects. The only constant was his consistent failure to regulate his meds. This was the thought that helped her to vindicate her next decision that this was fundamentally his own fault. Once this seed of an idea grew, it festered, putting the burn of anger in the pit of her stomach.

She pulled up Ray's message and hit REPLY.

Denise: When are you going to learn to take your meds? Get a taxi.

She hit SEND and dumped the phone in the glovebox.

Denise vacated her car and headed off to meet her stubborn, soon to be ex- lover.

CHAPTER TWENTY-SIX

Pulling into the parking bay, Brendan considered his night ahead with some trepidation. In his seventh-floor apartment on the outskirts of the city, an evening of Sky Box Sets and whiskey waited for him, and during those hours he would allow himself to become drunk and more self-pitying than at any other time since he'd lost Judith.

On the way home, his anger had given way to waves of despondency which washed over him, dragging him out and drowning him in a melancholic ocean. When he tried to focus on the 'whys and wherefores', he concluded that the nuances of the day had left him so emotionally *askew* that it was perhaps inevitable it would take its toll on his mood. He needed to consolidate, to regroup, and in order to kick-start the process, he needed the bottle of Bell's whiskey he'd stopped off for on the way back.

He parked up the Fiesta and retrieved the carrier bag holding his booze. He locked the car and headed towards his ten-storey tower block, a white and blue monolith, now turned grey and black in the streetlights. The locale was rough, but he was known well enough for people to accept him as someone who belonged there. Other than an occasional beggar and the local drunks trying to cadge the odd cigarette, he never had any bother.

He entered the block via a heavy steel door, garnished with a vertical slat of security glass, his electronic swipe card drawing a *ping* from the access panel. He ambled his way to the lifts. There were two of them, both entrances made from riveted steel, one for the even floors, and one for the odd.

Brendan smiled whenever he thought about climbing into the

'odd' lift. He figured it defined him and his life perfectly.

With a double-chime, the 'odd' car did indeed announce its arrival, and Brendan moved forward as the door slid open, all thoughts on getting to his seventh-floor flat where he would allow whiskey to soften his harsh thoughts of the world.

Two things went through his mind when he looked inside the lift: the first was the usual hope that no-one had pissed on the floor in the past hour, and the second—why the fuck was Eloise Adebola standing inside the car, waiting for him?

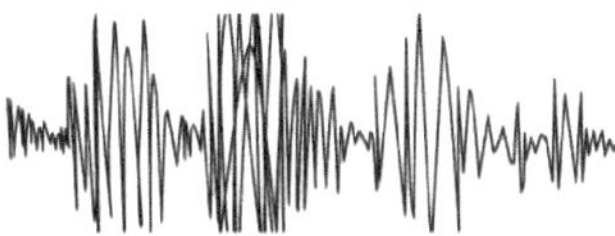

The taxi had been driving for over fifteen minutes before a thought traipsed through Ray's mind, a thought that had him swallowing hard with fear.

Denise might not even be at home.

He could feel anxiety turning his hands moist as he hit SETTINGS icon on his phone and found the heading for 'Find My iPhone'. Between them, he and his wife had lost two phones over the past few years, one left on a train when they spent their twentieth wedding anniversary in the London Savoy. The second, Denise had lost at one of her work events. Since that time, they'd agreed that the GPS location feature was to be their friend, and was a very good way of not crippling their annual insurance premiums. Such a thing relied on trust, of course; the service was only to be applied in absolute emergencies in order to avoid any suggestions of controlling or coercive behaviour on either of their parts. They were both absolute in this agreement, enough so that Ray still felt a sense of guilt as he now activated the setting.

He looked down at the map that came up on the screen and was surprised to see that the inverted red planchette representing Denise's phone was not indicating she was at home, but somewhere in Bromsgrove town centre. Ray zoomed in and found that the pin said the phone was somewhere on All Saints Road, a trunk road leading to the A38 that would take drivers out towards the nearby M42 and M5 motorways.

He leaned forward to address the taxi driver. "Hey, there. Can we head for All Saints Road, Bromsgrove?"

"It's your cash, mate," the driver replied cheerfully.

The taxi moved through the traffic, the agonising crawl through inner-city rush hour adding to Ray's frustration and anxiety. His finger beat out a tattoo on the armrest in the car door. This had the taxi driver turning up his radio, and incongruent, upbeat music from the Gurdwara Sikh temple filled the cab.

They drove on.

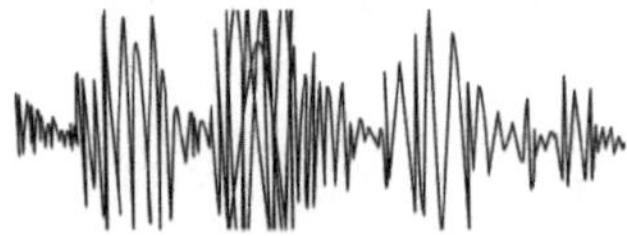

Gently, Mike carried his gift to the Mitsubishi 4x4 sitting on his drive, the hatchback already open to receive it. The creation in his arms was fresh, and remained quite delicate to the touch. He needed to make sure that there was no last-minute slip-ups. Everything depended on Eloise seeing how far he would go to protect her.

To protect them.

He lay the object down on a blanket, stroking strands of hair so they fell in place, and adjusted the clothing.

The last thing he did before closing the boot was to shut the eyes. If there was anything that unsettled him, it was the way his projects would stare back at him.

He was only human, after all.

CHAPTER TWENTY-SEVEN

"Come on, come *on*."

Ray's words were a mantra to frustration. The traffic through the city was sluggish as the taxi chugged its way through the choked streets. Streetlamps and headlights threw stark light on buildings that were now wet with rain, the windscreen wipers making intermittent squeaks as they fought to keep the glass clear of fat raindrops.

At a set of traffic lights, the car's interior became washed by the ruddy light from the stop sign. The taxi driver was wittering on about the latest football result, Ray catching something about Birmingham City being shit while West Bromwich Albion were infinitely better. Ray never quite got the appeal of the game. He kept rudimentary knowledge on scores and places in the league tables, and that was all. Such things helped for times like these, where they could be used to break the ice or maintain small talk with strangers. Otherwise, he considered the whole thing just ninety minutes of wasted time.

He peered out of the window and saw that they'd stopped by a line of shops. Directly opposite was a laundrette, where huge machines sat next to each other. He found himself drawn to a large machine facing him.

"Ray?"

A voice in the breeze. Soft, lilting.

"Denise?"

The day was turning sour. Like milk curdled by blood. He shivered.

"I'm so dirty."

Denise again, the Pied Piper on the wind, mesmerizing his senses, pulling him along as though he was a small fish on a very big hook.

"Oh, God, baby, where are you?"

He was no longer in the taxi, but rather standing in the launderette. The machines were squat, bright blue things trimmed with stainless steel. There were several, all in use, but one drew him in with ease. It drew him because of the blood, three vertical tracks of crimson breaching the rubber door seal.

Through its translucent, portal hatch, Ray could also see gore fizzing and foaming, thick crimson bubbles painting honeycomb patterns against the glass. He pressed his face against the machine door, trying to peer past the blood, trying to see his poor, poor Denise.

A hand slapped against the glass.

Denise's hand.

It was writhing—crimson and slick—the fingers working on finding purchase, the wedding ring tapping out its desperation. Desperately, Ray reached for it, placing his palm against the barrier. But Denise's hand failed in its attempt to find leverage and slid beneath the red, fizzing waves.

"No!" His fist beat upon the door, filling the air with heavy, dull sounds. "Denise!"

Then the face of his wife came into view, and his frustration turned to horror, pure and absolute. Denise was barely recognisable as the woman he'd loved for over twenty-five years. Her grey-white hair had turned to slimy, visceral tendrils slapped to her bloodied face as though she was enmeshed in thick, dark rope. One of her eyes was open, locked onto his, fear stamped into it. The other was gone, leaving a vacant socket that was periodically filling with a ghastly, gory bubble before popping, like a thick raindrop hitting the street.

The world winked out for a second, and the bloody vista went with it. The washing machine was a mere workhorse once more, full of pearly white suds, and he was back in the taxi.

Ray shook the image free of his mind and leaned towards the taxi driver. "Can't you go any faster?"

The man behind the wheel pointed at the line of red tail lights stretching out for what seemed like miles.

"Unless you want me driving down one way streets, this is our view for the next hour."

His frustration was building, almost blinding Ray with quiet rage. He felt his mind stir, then a sensation akin to a breeze passing over his skull. The taxi driver gasped, his hands now gripping the wheel, knuckles popping.

Ray leaned forward, his face level with the head rests of the front seat, his eyes on the 'One Way' and 'No Entry' signs on the side roads and alleyways.

"Just drive this fucking car," Ray hissed.

Without reservation, the driver obeyed.

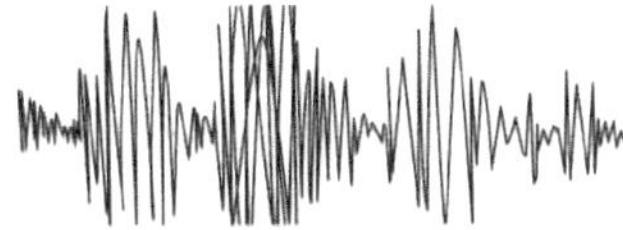

Eloise stood inside the elevator car, face impassive. Brendan stood on the threshold, clearly unsure of what was going on.

"Hello, Ellie," he eventually said. "Not seen you around here before. You got relatives in this block?"

"How about *you* tell *me* if I've got relatives here, Brendan?" she said smoothly. "It seems you've been taking an interest in every other aspect of my life over the past week."

"I'm not sure what you—"

"Stop. Do I look stupid to you? Is that what you think of me? That I'm a stupid little girl who doesn't know any better?"

He held up a placating hand. "No, of course not. I think you're very bright. And beautiful."

"What is this, Sunday School chorus?" she said sharply. "You've been following me around for days. And I want to know why."

The door to the lift began to close and Eloise put out a foot to activate the safety buffer. With noisy clatter, the door retracted back into its housing.

His response was sheepish, uncomfortable. "It's hard to explain. A little like how you found out where I lived."

She surprised him by stepping back into the lift to allow him access, her fingers resting on the control panel. "Well, I'll tell my story if you tell me yours."

Brendan stepped into the car, but his movements were sluggish and reluctant.

Eloise hit the button for the seventh floor.

"Going up," she said with a slight smile.

They rose through the belly of the building in silence.

CHAPTER TWENTY-EIGHT

In his haste to find his wife, Ray abandoned the taxi without paying, the driver staring straight ahead as though still in traffic. The trip out of the city had been interesting in a 'breaking every rule in The Highway Code' kind of way, their journey punctuated by reckless and dangerous driving, car horns and screeching tyres, one near miss after another added to their travel itinerary.

For Ray, there was no regret in his actions—these were desperate, frantic times. Sure, there would be repercussions, but that would be later, once Denise was safe. Until then, he simply didn't give a shit.

He emerged onto the street, scanning the surroundings for any sign of Denise's car.

The street was lined with office buildings, windows dark, their occupants long since headed off home or to the nearby town centre, where gastropubs and restaurants waited, warm and welcoming. To his left, there was a large car showroom, the lights still bright, throwing pools of brilliance on the wet pavement.

Across the road was a wide gateway with a sign saying it led to Blackfriars's Industrial Estate. He scanned the billboard with the logos of companies that had premises on site.

Something caught his eye.

There was a logo depicting a heraldic shield, with the image of a church and a run of steps leading up to the arched doorway. Over the doorway were two cartoonish gargoyles wrapped about each other. The company name was in a faux banner, and it read: Church & Shield Cosmetics LTD.

He couldn't explain the feeling that this was exactly the place he needed to be, any more than he could have explained his ability to see the terrible things he did. But the notion was so powerful, his feet were moving before realising he'd made the decision. His steps were slow at first, then gained momentum as an impending sense of dread clung to him like a heavy cloak.

As he made for the access gate, the thought that he'd have climb over it came to him. He slowed and scanned the perimeter, a line of high, deep hedges that he'd have no chance of scaling. Stepping up to the gates, he peered through the vertical bars, eyes alighting on something in the distance, a car illuminated by the high-powered lamps it was parked beneath.

An Audi A4.

His vision blurred as fear consumed him and Ray paused, waiting for the disorientating moment to pass. Yet the sensation escalated, the landscape about him becoming unstable until Ray stood on a vast, empty plane, the industrial estate winking out as though it had never existed. His limbs were immobile, a statue of flesh and bone.

The landscape was featureless, an endless expanse of grey sand. By contrast, huge, fat clouds reeled overhead, their colours vibrant and gaudy, swirling like paint poured onto grease. Like his body, his eyes were transfixed on the oleaginous sky, where hues churned, disturbed by great, winged beasts as they cruised the unfathomable heavens.

Day dream, he thought. *That's what this is, nothing but a bizarre day dream. Nothing to worry ab—*

The scream was sudden; so loud, shards of pain drove into Ray's ears. Instinct had him trying to raise his hands to clamp out the hideous din, but his arms remained at his sides, frozen. Mercifully, the shriek faded, replaced by a relentless ringing deep in his eardrum.

But there was something mixed with the hiss, a voice—whispered and insistent.

"See what is asked of you."

The ground beneath Ray's feet heaved, sending plumes of sand and ash skywards, showering him with grit. The sky broiled, its lurid colours churning to foam, making him feel nauseous. Even as he squeezed his eyes shut, his stomach lurched in time with the oscillating rocks underfoot.

Still a day dream. Still a fucking day dream!

"Behold!"

The voice again, bold and belligerent, and without his volition, Ray's eyelids snapped open as if pried by cruel, unseen fingers, the unveiled scene ahead leaving him agog.

A huge 'T' shaped structure had grown from the barren earth, the sand running from its horizontal limbs in dark cataracts, and Ray was reminded of crucified bodies robbed of blood. As terrible as this image was, he couldn't shake the feeling of wonder that came as grit and shingle fell away, revealing details beneath. The 'T' was imbued with ornate, confusing symbols, none of which he'd ever seen before; concentric cycles were melded with blunted triangles; stars and planets on the left limb were aligned and symmetrical, but on the right, they were askew, and held no discernible pattern.

"The adversary of order is chaos." The voice crawled through his ear, a parasite he was unable to ignore. "Watch!"

Ray gasped as a large platform descended on taut ropes from the right beam, and the incongruous sound of merry laughter and good cheer came to him. Then he saw them, people—too many to count, their faces smiling and their movements gregarious.

But as the platform continued its descent, the arm began to creak and started to drop with a squeal, and he noticed a rotating disc—a fulcrum—atop of the central column, shifting under the weight of the platform.

Scales, he realised. *A huge pair of scales!*

As the arm continued towards the ground, the demeanour of those on the dais changed, their merriment turning to cries of fear, and they clung onto one another, all waiting to be swallowed by the shivering, grey landscape.

Again, the great voice rasped on the thick, turgid air. "The adversary to chaos is order."

Another platform—this time from the left arm—but no laughter or cheer emanated from the writhing mob peering down at him. There was only rage and hate, grief and cursing, faces and bodies bloodied. Some fought each other, some hurt only themselves. It was a vile and pitiful sight, yet as the dais lowered, so too did the platform on the right-hand side start to climb, and as the people ascended, leaving behind the grey and unforgiving earth, they became joyful and resumed their celebration of life.

"What does this mean?" Ray yelled—to the people above, to the grey landscape. "What does it *mean*?"

But it was Denise he heard on the air. "Ray?" The timbre bubbled with thick liquid. "It's time."

Just as briskly as the scene came, so did it disappear, and Ray was back in the industrial estate, rain spattering his face, his stomach rolling with vertigo. He promptly vomited onto the tarmac, his back leaning forwards, his hands planted on his bent knees. Inside, panic began to climb. He fought to gain composure. Denise needed him. In some way, he feared the confounding vision was telling him her time was almost up.

Ray moved without further thought. The gate had a horizontal beam at its midsection and he heaved himself up and onto it, not caring if he was spotted by anyone passing. His fingers gripped the top of the gate and repeated the manoeuvre, carefully lifting one leg over the top of the frame and flattening out, looking like a jockey going for the last furlong. Then he brought over the next leg and unceremoniously clambered down the other side like some drunken abseiler. He jarred his ankle in the process, and he cried out in pain and annoyance.

Moving again, he headed off towards Denise's car, his right ankle throbbing in protest as he forced it to propel him onwards. At the Audi, he tried the door, but it was locked. He scanned the locale; several large warehouses loomed in the distance, their giant hulking shapes somewhat ominous in the yellow-grey light. To the right of the Audi was another building, where the huge hangar-like structure had been converted into several small units, each with their own reception area, accessed via a small door.

And one of these doors, in the unit nearest to Denise's vehicle, was outlined by the light coming from behind it. On the entrance was the 'Church & Shield Cosmetics LTD' logo. There was also something else coming from behind it, a dull rhythmic thud.

Ray headed for the door, pace quickening, not expecting for a moment to be able to gain access when he reached for the handle. Just as he'd thought, the lever held fast.

Now that he was closer to the unit, he could make out that the steady beat was some kind of drum. He recalled his vision on the train—the hideous creature in black, and the thumping din it beat out.

He began to shake with anger. Denise was inside with whatever had been haunting his visions. He knew this with such clarity it left him gasping as he clutched the door handle.

"For fuck's sake, open!" he hissed. The handle vibrated against his palm and static crackled, sending a shock through his fingers. He yanked his hand away and swore in surprise and pain. After a moment, he risked putting his fingertips back to the metal, tentatively testing it. When he realised the static shock had been discharged, he pushed down, and the handle yielded.

He shoved open the door, and inside, the reception was neat and tidy. There was a waiting area with several chrome and black seats, separated with small tables that contained magazines and leaflets. On the walls were posters and advertising for various cosmetics, perfumes and beauty products. The reception counter ran adjacent to the back wall. There was a small cash register and a black VD, and a bowl of purple crystal spheres rested to one side. Behind the counter, there was a plain white door, and it was ajar.

The dull drum beat was louder now, and Ray could also hear that it was accompanied by Gregorian chants, the sound of which almost stalled his heart. What the hell was going on here, and what the hell was this place? He laughed bitterly at his use of the term 'hell' when questioning visions filled with sinister, demonic figures, where chanting was now being added to the mix.

Hurrying onwards, the dull throb in his ankle reminded him that he needed to slow down. He'd considered phoning the police, but what was he to say? *Excuse me, Officer, but I have had a premonition my wife has been abducted by Satanists and is currently being held prisoner in a beauty product supply unit somewhere in Bromsgrove.*

It sounded stupid enough when he *thought* it, let alone when he had to do it for real. The only way to do this was to establish what was going on, and *then* call the police.

Another noise came to him, this time above the chanting and the drum beats. A loud moaning sound, as though someone was enduring great pain. It was enough to have him moving again, rushing behind the counter and over to the door. He peered through and saw that there was a large space, well-lit and lined with shelving units. His eyes took in the view, and the realisation that this was a stock area came shortly after.

The way looked clear, and he ducked inside, his ears following the thumps and chants as they came to him from deep within the stock room.

Using the aisles as cover, he crept through the space, and as he moved, he looked for anything he might use as a weapon. Unless any-one wanted a facial mask or foot spa, he couldn't see anything of use.

He reached the end of the long aisle and peered around the corner. He passed a service panel, a bulky grey box on one of the breezeblock walls. A large sticker with the silhouette of a man with a jagged dagger of electricity striking him down in mid-stride made clear that opening the cover with the power on was not a good idea. The words 'Danger of Death' below the image banged home the notion.

At the far end of the room was a short run of steps, at the top of which sat another door. Through this door came the sound of drums and chanting. The moan came again, this time rising in pitch until it was almost a scream.

Despite his battered ankle, Ray made for the steps. And before he realised it, he was crying out Denise's name.

CHAPTER TWENTY-NINE

"So, you want to start talking?"

Eloise was perched on the armrest of a small easy chair. She had a tumbler of whiskey in her hand, and she swirled the brown liquid in the glass, her eyes never leaving Brendan, who sat on a sofa that was covered in lime green velvet upholstery.

He had the bottle of booze at his feet. He'd already supped two glasses before he could even look at the woman sitting across the room. It had all seemed odd at first, but once the liquor was working on his brain, it felt like the right thing to do. Like a great burden was about to be lifted, just like it had when he'd told Judith his secret.

"I lost my partner a few years ago," he said quietly. "I think I got lonely. It grew from there. Things kind of got out of hand."

Eloise took a sniff at her drink and then pulled a face. "This smells as bad as your excuse. You know there's a law against stalking?"

Brendan looked up. There was a quiet panic in his eyes, but there was also something else, a glint of anger that betrayed the creature lurking beneath the remorse.

"That's *not* what I was doing, Ellie."

"Don't call me that," she said, her voice quiet, yet terse. "Only family and friends get to call me that, and you aren't either of those things."

They both sat in silence. Brendan took another gulp from his drink, emptying the glass. He reached for the bottle at his feet, but Eloise interjected by standing and walking over to him. She handed him her glass, which still contained all of her drink.

Her voice was languid. "You need this more than me, I think."

He took the glass from her. "So, what are you going to do?"

"I *could* call the police, tell them my suspicions. But what's the point? It's my word against yours, right?"

He mulled this over while staring at the drink she'd given him.

"I'm guessing this has more to do with *you*, than *me*," she finally said.

She still stood over him, her eyes never leaving his. They were dark and playful. He emptied her glass in three swallows before answering.

"The only way you'd have found out where I lived is by asking questions you had no business in asking, to people who shouldn't have answered," he said. "Who was it? My supervisor? A friend in HR?"

Her smile told him his assumptions had hit some kind of target.

"I found out, but I was subtle. Nothing traceable, because that would be the act of someone who didn't know what they were doing," she said. "And I know *exactly* what I'm doing, Brendan. Unlike you, I'm *careful.*"

Brendan shook his head as though trying to clear it. Eloise's voice was starting to break up, as though coming to him down a bad line. He lost sensation in his hands and the glass fell from his rubbery grasp, dropping to the carpet where it rolled to Eloise's feet. He suddenly realised she was wearing Croc shoes, the kind surgeons often wore in operating theatres.

"Slipped you a little Rohypnol, just to be on the safe side," she whispered. "A lady has got to be careful these days. You never know what *creeps* are out there, right?"

His eyes were glazed as he looked up at the woman still standing over him. As he fell into unconsciousness, he heard Eloise's voice through the maelstrom.

"Now then, dear Brendan, it's time to see what you're made of."

Mike drove his Mitsubishi into Eloise's road, his chest still tingling with anticipation. He'd played out the scenario in his head over a thousand times, enticing Eloise out of her home and to his vehicle, where he would introduce her to his creation.

He was trembling with excitement when he thought about how she might react when she first saw it. The emotional response was important to this whole event, setting the wheels in motion for the next phase. He couldn't think about *that* right now—the exhilaration such a thought produced was almost overwhelming. But he knew that if things went to plan, the investment would have been worth it.

The things that brought great pleasure always were.

Eloise's address was accessed via a run of terraced houses that terminated in a cul-de-sac. A semicircle of eight detached homes, each with their own drive, was lit by streetlamps. The darkness beyond the rooftops appeared oppressive, the huge shadows of clouds crossing the sky hinting at a storm.

Mike pulled the car into the cul-de-sac and scanned the windows of Eloise's house. They were all dark, making clear that no one was at home. He felt his frustration rising. Could nothing *ever* go right for him? Was he destined *not* to connect with her?

He had considered calling first, but decided against it. When he thought about the decision now, he began to worry if it was a huge mistake not to phone ahead. The most obvious issue was that he wanted to surprise her, gauge the reaction to his 'gift'.

But the reality was that he'd been scared to call, in case she made it clear she didn't want him to visit. That would have made things awkward going forward, because then it would have felt as though he was being insistent if he'd shown up after such a rebuke.

He hated feeling like this. The confusion and doubt around women was emotionally crippling; it made him feel vulnerable. When such sentiments bled into his psyche, his natural response was to shut down. This led to closing off the cause of the upheaval to the point of evasion, and that didn't exactly create prosperous working relationships, let alone romantic ones.

Romantic.

He chuckled as the word dropped into his head. Life wasn't like it was in the movies, as much as he wanted it to be. There were no 'happy ever afters', there were only realities and chosen moments that either went your way, or didn't.

With this thought in mind, Mike had decided that it was time to take control and make those moments count. And this had suddenly felt as right as making the piece he now had stowed in the boot.

He turned off the headlights, settled back in his seat, and waited for Eloise to return.

CHAPTER THIRTY

Ray ploughed into the room without stopping, the door swinging in with ease, and he almost fell to his knees as the momentum caught him out. He clutched onto the door handle as he took in the scene inside the room, and had he not been using the door for support, his legs would have ultimately betrayed him, as they'd suddenly become rubber beneath him.

At first, Ray couldn't determine what it was he *actually* saw, his mind bombarded with multiple images at once. There were three figures in the room. A deathly pale shape lay on a large mattress on the floor. It was a woman, blonde and naked, her body unblemished, giving the appearance of a blanched corpse. He gawped as he recognised the pursed mouth, the white goo dribbling from her lips. Her eyes were staring at the ceiling, her breasts pert, defying gravity, and somewhere in Ray's mind, a conclusion was drawn.

A sex doll. High quality, but a sex doll all the same.

Elsewhere, the walls were covered in some hideous paisley motif, gold images on a blood red background, and in the flickering candle-light, these gilded patterns seemed to writhe like hideous, bloated plants, their tubers covered with gilded boils.

Then he saw the other figure, clad head to foot in black leather, the seams stitched together with silver thread. In its hand was a faux whip, curled like a tentacle, snaking to the floor.

And the final figure was bound to a saltire cross with leather thongs. It wore only a loose white ball gown, marred by a single tyre track. He also saw that the material was smeared red, as were the ankles and wrists of the person tied to the cross. The face was covered with a

Bellissima Masquerade Mask, and in the back of his mind, Ray began to think about cartons of pink milk and severed heads. No surprise on the latter as he looked at the gore on the limbs of the crucified figure.

Blood, he thought, *the whole body covered in blood.* But something didn't ring true. And then it hit him, the level of incredulity at what he could see, the sudden horror now beginning to wane, giving way to confusion as the smell hit him.

A mixture of perfume, sweat and...

The heady smell of strawberries hit him, and he recalled the cloying scent from his previous visions. He cast his eyes to the bottle of Hershey's sauce lying on the floor at the foot of the cross. The realisation came to him, and he allowed it to flood out, regardless of the hurt it brought to his heart.

Not blood.

Not pain.

Not death.

None of those things. Instead: gimps and strawberries and bondage, ecstasy and betrayal.

"Oh, shit," the person beneath the mask breathed. Ray recognised the voice of his wife instantly, and coldness descended upon him.

The figure in black turned and Ray looked upon the gimp mask, the stitches and zipper-eyes no longer terrifying and sinister, but lurid and ludicrous.

"What the hell are you doing in here?" the zippered face said.

Ray's words oozed out, and with them, he once more felt his mind help them along. "Leave. Now. Close the door on your way out."

At his command, the figure in black stood to attention, as if the idea were his own. "Sure. Okay."

"Peter!" Denise yelled. "Don't leave me like this!"

"Peter?" Ray said softly, and the man paused and took a step backwards, as though he'd bumped into an invisible wall.

"Yes?"

"Go and find the stars, Peter," Ray breathed. "Go and be with them."

"Yes," Peter said, voice robotic. "Yes, I'd like that."

"Off you go," Ray said.

Peter walked from the room as though in a trance. He even closed the door behind him, as Ray had suggested.

Ray walked over to a portable speaker at the base of the mattress and turned off the hideous chanting music. The silence that followed was total and, in some ways, much worse.

He looked about him—at the love doll on the mattress, the video camera with a screen that was a hissing static haze, and his wife, still on her pretend cross, her head turned away from him in humiliation.

Ray went over and stood, looking up at her. The moments rolled out, neither of them able to say a word.

It was Denise who finally called an end to the silence. "I told him it was over, but he wouldn't listen. He had the earring and used it to coerce me here. Said he'd tell you everything if I didn't." She didn't look at him. He assumed she wasn't quite ready for that yet.

"Does it matter?" he said flatly.

"Yes," she said, her voice dulled by her mask. "It does. Get me down from here and we can talk."

"Talk?"

"Yes. About how it's come to this."

"What?" It came out as an incredulous laugh. Oh yes, he'd really like to know how it had come down to his wife being mock-crucified by a man in a gimp mask and doused in fucking strawberry syrup.

But not now. Not when rage bubbled in his gut. Not when his life was about to fall apart.

"Ray, please," Denise whimpered as she finally turned to look at him. "Let me try to explain. Let me try to fix this."

But it was now he who turned away, putting a trembling hand to his mouth in an attempt to smother the sob that so badly wanted out. He left the room before it became too difficult to bear, only just making it to the bottom of the steps, where it came out hot and angry.

He balled his fists and pummelled the walls with such fury, a box of hair extensions crashed to the floor. Anger and hate came in an emotional tsunami that threatened to sweep him away into oblivion.

Denise's voice came to him from the room above, a desperate cry for him to come back and set her free. She said words like 'sorry' and 'forgiveness', but they were lost to his cold temper.

Before he could stop it, in that churning, swirling place, a thought rose up like a primordial leviathan beating back the waves—what if that strawberry syrup wasn't syrup at all? What if it was blood, and his beloved, betraying wife was lying in it, bathing in it, her chest and abdomen pulled apart like a cheap carpet bag?

It was the briefest of things, there for a mere moment. But it was soon gone.

Then, the screams began.

CHAPTER THIRTY-ONE

A great fog swirled before Brendan's eyes, and this eerie mist wasn't affiliated with just his vision, it clouded his brain—his consciousness—creating a disorientating shroud that prevented him from understanding anything that was going on. Something called to him through the gloom, sullying his psyche, something bright and insistent. Not a light, but something just as potent.

The sensation became more urgent, persistent, and, like a hand dragging him through broiling water, he was hauled from his fugue and into the here and now. And no sooner had he become aware did he understand that his calling had come from the exquisite agony now being inflicted upon his body.

Eyes wide, he saw that his naked torso was raked and bleeding, his arms and feet pinned to the kitchen table with knives hammered through his ankles and palms. He gave out a huge scream as the pain took him, but it was stalled in his throat by a piece of material that tasted of salt and stank of urine. Somewhere in his mind he recognised the possibility that this was, in fact, his own underwear, before his butchered body insisted he pay it some attention.

Standing over him, Eloise smoothed out the kitchen apron with hands covered with bright yellow kitchen gloves. The apron and the gloves were wet with gore—his gore—and the smile on Eloise's face was no longer subtle—it was a leer that was at once serene and evil.

"Hush now, Brendan," she whispered. "This is what you wanted, remember? You wanted to feel *alive*, and there is no greater feeling of life than the moment before death. I know it. I have seen it, in the eyes of those who have felt steel and lost blood."

Brendan whimpered, his mind threatening to leave him at any moment, and in truth, this would not have been a bad thing. Eloise leaned over him so that her dark eyes loomed close. They looked like the eyes of a shark, and he did not doubt that her capacity for mercy was as comparable.

"But you have such a special place in this story," she said. "You are a predator, and this makes us the same. It is a powerful thing, this connection, and I am giddy with it. I've never felt such a thing before. It's all in the *eyes*, Brendan. Usually, I take the eyes last, when the fun is over. But yours are so, so special. You are defined by what you have seen, my friend, and there is no recompense for such a gift. So, I feel I have no choice but to take them *first,* and keep them forever. You understand, of course. Deep down, I *know* you do."

Despite the excruciating pain his endeavours incurred, Brendan tried to move his impaled limbs, his head thrashing from side to side, his underpants still turning his desperate cries to muted growls at the back of his throat.

He squeezed his eyes shut, trying to make the inevitable difficult. But even as he did so, he could not erase the last image he'd seen of Eloise Adebola as she'd raised a yellow, gloved hand, and the glittering dessert spoon she clutched within it.

There had been some form of bridge in the City of Worcester since Anglo-Saxon times, but it was not until the late 11th century that one of significance was constructed to span the river Severn at the north-western corner of the original town. It was a place of prominence, given that it was the only crossing between the towns of Gloucester and Bridgenorth, sixty-eight miles apart.

There had been several iterations since, the times and materials determining the structure's strength, prominence, and, of course, its history, including civil and world wars.

Now, in the 21st century, completely unaware of its checkered history, Peter Cound stood on the bridge, his bodysuit and zippers reflecting the yellowed street lights. As with most things in his life, he'd no idea how he'd got here. His VW was parked illegally across the street, the driver's door thrown wide open. His mind was in a daze, only vaguely aware that his attire was so out of keeping with his surroundings. But not enough to care. He may have been here, but he wasn't quite *present*.

In his mind were fleeting memories, snapshots of recent events that emerged like koi carp feeding on the surface of a still lake. He looked at the surging waters below. God, how he loved the way the black, black surface sparkled, as though the night sky had fallen to Earth.

He tried to piece his thoughts together, figure out exactly what had happened, how the hell he'd found his way here. There was his affiliation with the area, of course. He'd been born eight or so miles away in Great Malvern, with the iconic hills on his doorstep. He pictured the cottage where he'd grown up, a sedate place with educationalist parents that were simple in their outlook, neat and orderly in how they conducted themselves, both at home and to the outside world. His was a wholesome upbringing, safe, and—until he'd met Sandy, his wife—very predictable.

The first sign that Sandy had preferred a more exotic approach in the bedroom occurred a few months after they'd been sleeping together. Trust, he was to find out, was intrinsic to the sexual lifestyle he was to adopt in the coming years. Once Sandy knew she could do exactly that, she told him of her proclivity for being tied up, and for him to *enjoy* her submissiveness. He loved her, so went along with the request, initially feeling a little odd as he did exactly as she asked, watching her sexuality come to life.

To his surprise, the experience was equally as intense for him. He enjoyed the control, a release from the chaos of a busy work life. The games progressed over the years, becoming complex, the psychology far more sophisticated. Role play, toys, suits and bondage masks, the whole gambit shaping a life that, despite what outsiders may have thought, was still based in deep love and total trust.

When Sandy had their two children—twin boys, Sean and Edward—Peter agreed with her that parenthood had to come first. And they did exactly that, waiting until the kids were of an age to be left with grandparents for a night or two. Their games could begin again, heightened by such a period of abstinence. Life, it seemed, was perfect.

Perfect, that was, until the day that Sandy began having headaches so severe she was left bedbound for days. Tests were ordered by her GP, but in the interim, she'd fallen foul to a massive seizure while Peter was downstairs making some supper for them both. By the time he'd returned to the bedroom, he found that Sandy had choked on her tongue. She'd been dead for over fifteen minutes.

The twins were teenagers, and Peter was a grieving widower at forty-five. Grief bit hard, as did the guilt of being downstairs cooking when he should have been there when his dear wife needed him the most. Close family got him through, especially the collective grandparents of his two boys.

Fatherhood dominated the next five years, the emotional wellbeing of his sons usurping anything else in his life. As grief loosened its jaws, the savage sting becoming a dull ache in the heart, Peter saw his sons flourish. Sean became a doctor; Edward, a lawyer. His own career as a quality improvement lead had been put on hold for a while, but his aptitude for organisational change was such that he was able to rejoin and rebuild his work life. But there remained a huge gap in his wellbeing—a companion who shared his penchant for sexual exploration.

He'd almost got to the point where he was having to accept such opportunities were never going to come his way again. But then came a chance meeting with someone in whom he saw the need for control, someone with whom he felt an immediate connection.

Denise.

It had been wonderful, their liaisons together. They cared for each other—he *knew* it, deep down, even though she'd never told him as such. He wasn't looking to replace Sandy; there didn't need to be love, absolute. There just needed to be trust and respect, a safe and nurturing environment where they could explore each other's desires.

But things have gone wrong, haven't they, his mind said briskly. *You broke the basic and most important rules of the game.*

He swallowed hard, but the sensation was distant, as though the act was procured by someone else. In a recess of his mind something nudged at him, an irreparable *blackness* that had his heart turning to iced water.

By contrast, his thoughts were a raging lava.

In your haste to sequester your own needs, you lost sight of the most intrinsic law of BDSM, didn't you? You forgot about mutual consent. You forgot about respect and trust.

He could deny it all he wanted, but he knew this was all true. He'd used subterfuge on day one, when he'd lied about his wife leaving him and having a son and daughter. Building a story to bait the trap for a vulnerable, caring woman to step into. Using the earring to coerce Denise into continuing the game, taking photographs without her permission, threatening to use them—all of this was fundamental, a breach of the very protocols designed to prevent abuse.

It was desperation on his part. The fear of losing such a willing partner was almost as bad as—

No, not as bad as losing Sandy, but close. So, so close; enough for him to be rash, and extend his control beyond their safe space, out into the world.

Without agreement. Without sanction.

That black, black place in his brain began to bleed into his mind, into his thinking, turning everything to oil. He saw Denise, on that cross, the muddy, white ball gown, the syrup and toys, but they were being absorbed by that oppressive, indefatigable darkness. All he could picture was a fathomless pit of guilt and despair, and these awful emotions had him seeking any form of solace.

His throat hitched, tears falling. He peered down, those sparkling, spangled lights danced upon the churning water, mesmerising. Beckoning like stars.

Demanding.

He had little choice but to join them.

CHAPTER THIRTY-TWO

Eloise's car showed up two hours after Mike had parked in the cul-de-sac. He saw the headlights approach, the beams dazzling after so long sat in the streetlamp twilight. He didn't realise it was her until she manoeuvred the Fiat onto her driveway. Motion-activated porchlights came on in an explosive flare, flooding the driveway in stark white.

She'd opened her car door and was fishing in her handbag as Mike walked up to her, saying a hushed 'hi' as he did so as not to startle her.

Despite his fears, Eloise didn't appear to be alarmed by his presence at all. In fact, she gave him a smile that was made radiant by the porchlights.

"Well, this is a surprise," she said softly.

Mike appeared bashful. "Yeah. Sorry to disturb you at this time of night. I've got something to show you."

She giggled. "You know how wrong that sounds?"

He smiled, but it was laced with uncertainty. "Oh, yeah. Sorry. I meant that I made you something. Something *special*."

Eloise's eyes widened. "Really? And what have you made for me?"

Mike enjoyed seeing the playful look on her face. "You want to come to the car? It's in the boot."

"You really *are* a tease. You're lucky that I like secrets."

"Are you good at keeping them, though?" he asked.

"No, I'm terrible. Most of the time I tell people and have to kill them afterwards."

Mike chuckled, and she joined in.

She walked up to him. "So, are you going to show me what you've made?"

To Mike's surprise, she linked arms with him and steered him towards his car. He popped open the boot, and the interior lights revealed the figure inside.

The face was framed by ringlets of blonde hair, frozen in neutral. The interior lights of the Mitsubishi's boot space gave the exposed cheeks and brow a sallow sheen, turning the lips blue-black, the wide, staring eyes almost coal-coloured. There was a long, flowing dress, arms lying across the lower abdomen and delicate fingers of the right hand resting on top of the left. There were frills and petticoats and black, patent shoes with silver buckles.

Eloise gasped with delight. "Oh, Mike, this is beautiful. Did you really make it all by yourself?"

He nodded, and his face was sheepish with embarrassment.

"This is amazing," she said as she traced her fingers over the silky-smooth surface. "You have a great gift."

She turned, went up on her tiptoes, and gave him a kiss on the cheek. It was slow and exquisite. "Thank you."

"You're welcome," he said, his voice hushed. "I'm pretty embarrassed that I'm able to do this kind of thing. I've never told anyone about it before. But it somehow gives me great peace, you know?"

"You're very thoughtful. How about you go and take our little friend into my lounge. I'm almost too afraid to pick her up. She looks like she might break."

"She's very sturdy now everything has set properly," he said. "But I can carry her through."

"Does she have a name?" Eloise asked.

"Only her owner can name her. That's how it has to be."

"Then I shall name her Tiffany. It was my mother's name."

"That sounds perfect," he said. He scooped the tiny body out of the car and carried it to Eloise's porch, where she opened the front door before standing aside and allowing him access.

"Go to the right," she said. "You can put her in the lounge. She can keep watch over me on these long winter nights."

Mike did as he was asked and set the figure down on a sideboard, adjusting the legs so that it stood upright, the glassy eyes surveying the lounge. He finished up by tousling the curls, giving them volume. He stepped back and admired his handiwork for a final time.

The doll looked back at him, the gaze as expressionless as they always were when he'd set them in their final resting place. For a moment he recalled the first time he lined up his first three pieces, photographing them in order to get admission to the Dollmaker's Guild. It was a proud moment, one that finally had him appeasing the guilt of what he'd done to his own mother's precious doll when he'd destroyed it in his teenage tantrum.

Sensing Eloise beside him, he looked over at her. Just like the newly christened Tiffany, he saw that her face was deadpan, as though she was thinking about something profound.

"Ellie? Are you okay?"

At his voice, she seemed to come back from wherever her mind had taken her, and the smile returned to her face.

"You seemed far away."

"More than you'll ever truly know. Would you like a drink?"

Mike paused before answering. "Of course, thank you."

"It's the least I can do," she said, disappearing into the kitchen. "Scotch okay?"

"Absolutely," he said, his shoulders relaxing a little. He gave Tiffany a small wink.

Within a few minutes, Eloise had returned with two glasses.

She handed him his drink and went back to the doll, lifting the hem of its skirts in order to examine the craftwork.

"Such exquisite stitching," she said with a sigh. "I'm always fascinated by the art of needlework. There is something about how thread can pull together that which is torn asunder, don't you think?"

She saw the smile on Mike's face telling her that he understood all too well. But she knew he couldn't *really* understand. How could he?

Maybe if he had seen Eloise looking down into the open casket of her father at the funeral director's parlour all those years ago, studying the peaceful face on display. Maybe if he had felt the surge of love she felt in the moments when her hands smoothed out her father's best silk shirt, and the feeling of something beneath the fabric, the hard ridge that had inquisitive hands popping open the buttons and peering beneath, where the puckered flesh had been sutured a little too tightly. Little four-year-old Ellie and the grieving mind of her older self fused the elements of love, life and death in those moments as effectively as the stitches pulled together her father's dead flesh to create an autopsy scar.

She would later look up the embalming process and learn that all the components of life were removed in order to present a person for death. Her father was empty in a physical sense, internal organs gone, while the daughter he left behind had been gutted by grief.

Somewhere in the sociopathic dynamic, it made sense that she should yearn to *collect* things from time to time; things to fill her own psychological void. Since the loss of her father, she had felt dismantled, and her only solace was the moments when she claimed something from the living to make her feel complete, to help cope with death. She would never question it, nor would she ever consider it abhorrent. It was, just like the doll she now looked upon, born from a skewed sense of love.

Her time in this town was going to have to come to an end. She knew that she may have been a little too frivolous over the past few hours; it was time to move on. Still, she had these moments, and in them, she felt contentment.

She allowed the hem to fall, moving closer to Mike as he finished off his drink. Reaching down, she took his big hands in hers; his fingers trembled with anticipation—or perhaps it was the Rohypnol in his drink kicking in.

Looking down at Mike's palms, a small smile came to Eloise's lips.

"What's the matter?" he whispered. His breathing was becoming rapid, and his eyes appeared glassy, as though he were becoming a doll himself.

She gazed up at him, her eyes sparkling with dark desire. "You know, Mike, if only I could *own* hands like these. I believe I would treasure them *forever*."

CHAPTER THIRTY-THREE

"So, you found your wife," Cross asked. "Then what happened?"

"You *saw* what happened, detective."

Oh yes, Cross had seen it, all right. Twenty minutes after the fact, when a calm and placid Ray Tonks had called to say that he'd murdered his wife and that the police needed to come right now, because there was *so much blood.*

By the time Cross arrived, the cops responding to the call were outside the industrial unit, puking on the asphalt. Once he'd been inside, the detective could understand why. Mrs Tonks had been crucified and taken apart, like ripe fruit exploding on the pavement. In twenty years of policing, the detective had never seen anything like it. But one thing was for sure: it was the work of fury. *A crime of passion,* the French would say, but Cross could only see wholesale slaughter, committed by a husband who confessed he was so consumed with jealousy he'd torn his wife to pieces.

The question was: *How?*

"I am a walking, talking metaphor. A joke, some might say."

"There's no joking in any of this, Ray. Your wife was eviscerated and left to hang like a lamb in a butcher's shop window."

"Left on display as a martyr for the ills of the world. At my behest.

Surely that alone is enough to condemn me?"

"There is no evidence. You know this. The damage inflicted on Denise was significant. Our pathologists say it was done while she was still alive. There would have been blood splatter on your clothing."

It was everywhere else, Cross' errant mind thought.

Ray seemed to be looking through him, making the detective inwardly shudder. He had a feeling he may have to play *two* Rammstein records before going home tonight.

"Yes," Ray said. "Yes, there was *lots* of blood. Incredible how much a body can hold. I wouldn't have believed it if I hadn't seen it for myself. How a body just *collapses* when it's emptied of its innards. Remarkable."

Cross leaned forward. "Yet, like I said, not one drop on *you*."

"I told you, detective. In my temper, the thought got away from me, and it became true. This is what I now offer to our world."

Cross frowned. "The CPS isn't going to buy that, Ray."

Ray shrugged. "Then why not say I wore protective gear? Stuff I disposed of after I *did the deed?*"

"There's no evidence of that either. You *were* at the scene. You called it in. We can put you there, you have motive, but there's just no evidence that you laid a finger on your wife. All the evidence points to the work of someone else. And, for some reason, you want to take the blame for it. Maybe you feel guilty because there was a moment when you *wanted* to hurt Denise. After you found out what was going on. It's human nature, I guess. But I don't know for sure, that's psychologist territory. The only prints and DNA at the scene belong to your wife and her lover, Peter Cound, and that makes *him* our number one suspect."

"No," Ray said, his voice taut. "This crime is mine, and mine alone."

Cross continued regardless. "We'll keep on looking, although as of now, Cound has disappeared off the face of the Earth."

"Yes," Ray ceded whimsically. "He's gone to be with the stars. I *was* at the scene. I have described to you what happened. You need only listen to see my guilt."

"Sorry, Ray. There's simply no case against you."

Cross watched Ray slump back in his seat, dejected. He continued, rambling with closed eyes as if Cross wasn't even in the room.

"If I had known it would be this hard to be arrested, maybe I'd have left *more* evidence. I was just too shocked, see? The visions were just metaphors, a defence mechanism, a means to stop me from interfering with what fate had planned for us all. Can you believe that? Even in this madness, there are still *rules*."

Ray's eyes flicked open, and Cross found that he was now looking at a man teetering on the brink of madness.

"I thought about putting an end to this," Ray said, mouth askew. "If the law can't find a way to punish me, then maybe I could open up my wrists in my cell when I'm left with my dinner cutlery. You'd be surprised by how effective plastic knives can be when they're put to use with a little determination. Instead, I opted for a shirt sleeve," he touched the wheal on his neck. "Fat lot of good that did."

"Perhaps your heart wasn't really in it?" Cross offered, gently. "Maybe it's because, deep down, you can't convince yourself that you actually did this to your wife. Maybe it's a hopelessness thing. This isn't your fault, Ray. No one could have seen this coming. No matter what your mind says, you did *not do this*."

Cross saw the cold calm return to Ray's face. "*Circumstantial*, right?"

"Exactly."

A small growl of frustration came from the back of Ray's throat. "If you think all of this happened on a whim, you're a fool," Ray said, bluntly. "You see, there's no such thing as *chance*, Malcolm. This power isn't a gift. I can see that now with a sense of clarity that would leave you gibbering in fear. My ability comes with an overwhelming sense of purpose. And at great cost."

Cross tried to smooth the frustrated edge creeping into his voice. "And what *is* its purpose, Ray?"

"Balance."

The detective drew in a breath, then let it go, slow and steady. "I don't understand."

"I'm not surprised. I didn't at first," he giggled, and Cross found the sound intimidating. But Ray continued, "But can you think about the universe, how fucking *vast* it is?"

"Yes."

Ray nodded, eyes twinkling, awestruck. "Now imagine the space between each star as other universes, light and dark all going about their business, neither knowing about the other. But *something* does. Something connects them all."

Cross sighed. "Are you talking about God again, Ray?"

Ray slapped his hand on the table, and despite his training, Cross flinched.

"That's too *simple*, Malcolm. It trivialises the scale of this thing. What I'm saying is that good and bad things occur, they co-exist— in time and space—but in order for that to happen, there has to be *equilibrium*. The universe must be kept *stable*."

Cross held up a placating hand. "Ray, listen to me, I'm not sure—"

"You're not listening!" Ray's anger was barely contained. Cross could see veins pulsating at the man's temples. "I'm part of a mechanism by which the cosmos achieves balance, Malcolm. The scales, remember? I told you about the scales! For all the good things that happen, there must be bad. That is my purpose."

Cross replied softly—an attempt to pacify Ray's fervent ire. "But you've not committed any crime."

But Ray pressed on without acknowledging the detective's statement. "It's hard to fathom, isn't it, the scale of such power? But I'm still a small cog. There are many like me, out there in the cosmos, doing this vile work. Slaves to it."

"If that's the case, then why now?" Cross said, trying to inject reason into the madness.

Ray thought this over, his eyes looking to the fluorescents as though their brilliance held the answer. After a short time, he nodded to himself.

"I'm mere matter, a child of the stars—as are we all. To be given this power in its purest form would have fried my body like an egg in hot oil. So it was introduced over time, until it became the very fabric of who I am."

"And what are you?"

"The trite would call me *karma*. But that is a word begat by human beings, forever searching for meaning, for truth."

Cross struggled with the words. "So, you're saying that for every good thing going on in the universe, you must endure the bad?"

"If only it were that simple. Perhaps I would at least have a rationale to offer myself some comfort."

"Then what *are* you saying?"

"I'm the harbinger of misfortune, Malcolm," Ray said. "Every bad deed or event that happens in this world will soon be at my behest."

"You cannot believe that?" But Cross saw in Ray's face that he did believe it, total and absolute.

"Tonight, I've embraced that which was given. Denise was the conduit for acceptance. I tried to fight it, but we know how that turned out once I felt the wrath of betrayal. Now my body is no longer unstable. I'm changing. But there is still time."

"Time?" Cross asked, bewildered.

"I'm straddling worlds—in transition, if you will. Not yet dis-corporeal," Ray explained. "You can still end this. You can do your duty and be my saviour."

But Cross resisted. "That doesn't make sense, Ray."

"I can't kill myself," Ray replied, exasperated. "If I try, I black out before I even get chance to act. Every. Single. Time. The cosmos *needs* me to survive. I'm set on a path upon which there is no turning back.

"I realise now, these past weeks, I have been witness to dealings that weren't mine to see, private lives of others. Skewed lives, some that I think may have had evil intent. They were mere snapshots, happening so fast I convinced myself I was having intrusive thoughts. Now I *know* terrible things have happened. This is the shape of things to come, if you want a cliché, Malcolm. This is my place in things. I can feel *everything*. The pain, the fear, the guilt, the ecstasy, the peace. Not for me, you understand. No, no peace *at all*. Now, I'm no longer meant to observe. I'm to *influence* events, shape them, in order to maintain order in the cosmos. Yes, it may have great meaning, it may serve esteemed purpose, but *no* man has such a right. No man *deserves* such a right. I don't want it. I need to be free of it before it consumes me forever. Will you help me?"

The desperation in Ray's voice was palpable, and Cross *did* feel for him. But at that moment there was simply nothing he could do, even with Ray's unreasoned ramblings.

"I'm sorry, Ray. Like I've said, there's no evidence to suggest you had a hand in killing Denise. Besides, even if you were locked away forever, what good would it do? By your own logic, I can't see how these powers you say you have would be contained."

Ray's fingers traced the edge of the table. "You're right, of course. But being charged for my wife's murder is balance for *me*, Malcolm. An acknowledgement that what I have done is evil, no matter what the intent."

Malcolm shrugged. "I'm not sure I accept that argument, Ray. But it's irrelevant at this point. Like I say, my hands are tied. I'm going to have to release you."

Ray closed his eyes and took in a deep breath. He exhaled slowly, deliberately, and when he opened his eyes again there was a sense of calm—a realisation, clear and bright.

"Then I guess I'm going to have to *do* something to make the charges stick," he said softly. "You are all my witnesses. I pray that when all is said and done, you shall become my executioner. You will become God in my final moments, Detective. You will recognise evil and punish my sin."

Before Cross could quiz him, Ray had once again closed his eyes.

There was a sudden, dull thud against the one-way glass panel. From the corridor beyond the interview room, shouts and screams came sharp, despite the distance.

Cross jumped to his feet. "What the fuck have you done?"

"What use are eyes if you refuse to see the truth?" Ray sighed.

"Stay here," Cross said as he went to the door.

Ray said nothing. He let his smirk speak for him.

Cross unlocked the door, and no sooner was he outside did his eyes see only chaos, but his mind did not immediately understand what was actually happening.

There were several people in the corridor, some uniformed officers, some in civilian clothes. A police constable was sitting on the floor, head in his hands, crying out for his mother. A female detective Cross knew as Charlotte Warren staggered about the corridor, hands outstretched, fingers wriggling in the air as though reaching out for something she could not see.

Charlotte's eyes were weeping, and when Cross looked upon her, he saw that her eyeballs were bone white, irises and pupils all stripped away.

Another male police officer shambled through the scene, tripping over the outstretched legs of the person sitting on the floor and crashing into Charlotte. Both collapsed, hitting the linoleum hard.

Cross put a hand to his mouth in horror. *All blind*, he realised.

"What use are eyes if you refuse to see the truth?"

Ray's words came to him again, and when he saw their meaning first hand, Cross felt anger course through him. He turned and went back to the interview room, finding that Ray hadn't moved from his seat. Nor had the smirk left his face.

"None so blind as those that will not see, Malcolm."

"Okay, you've made your point," Cross hissed. "Stop this now. Put things back the way they were."

Ray shook his head. "There's no turning back the clock. There is only what you can do to stop my place in the future. I can't end it. I've tried."

Cross scowled. "What the hell are you?"

"I *told* you what I am. I am the abyss. I am the void. I am the false prophet who brings only a future of pain. The question is, what are *you* going to do about it? This is your call, Detective. 'Protect and Serve' the public. What must I do to make you *do your duty?* You are a family man, after all. Time to save all you hold dear, I think."

Cross appeared to sway as realisation took him. "Don't you dare," he whispered.

"I can feel your wife and daughter on the ether," Ray crooned.

"Shall I take their eyes, too?"

Cross reached inside his jacket, pulling the telescope baton from the sheath on his belt. He extended it with a flick of his wrist.

"You leave my family alone, Ray," he spat.

"Then do what you must, detective. Or your fate will be mine."

Ray placed his head down on the table, forehead pressing against the wooden surface, his whole demeanour passive.

"You will become God in my final moments, Detective. You will punish my sin. Send me back to the abyss. Before it's too late."

Ray's words felt so right at that moment, Cross couldn't believe why he was even having trouble deciding what needed to be done.

Despite there being no one left in the station to see what he was about to do, Cross still turned and closed the interview room door behind him.

Then, he did his duty.

END

AUTHOR NOTES

Here begins the story of a story.

False Prophet is a tale that has, over time, seen more than its fair share of change. The premise came after watching a TV showing of telekinetic horror film The Medusa Touch (1978) starring the late, great Richard Burton, and based on the 1973 novel by Peter Van Greenaway. At that point, I was an impressionable early teen from a Black Country council estate with dreams of writing and drawing comic books for a living. Reality came home to roost pretty soon thereafter. I sucked as an artist and numerous rejections from publishers had me thinking similar things about my writing. Shortly before wrapping up the dream for a fair few years (and seeking a day job that ultimately became a fulfilling 35 year career), I wrote two short stories in the same week. The first was called Devil of a Deal(later retitled To the Devil his Due in my self-published chapbook, Gargoyle Grotesque). The second story was I've Seen Things You'd Never Believe, later retitled Foresight for another short-lived, self-published outing. Short-lived because I was never really happy with the story, always feeling that it had more to say, with a need for more characters in order to effectively say it. Thus, I shaped the core concepts of a longer novella under the title 'Bad Vision'. This novella may have progressed the story and added more characters, but only in False Prophet—with its extensive, additional character depth, and several brand new story arcs thanks to editorial discussions with Eerie River Publications—can I finally say that this tale is as I intended to tell it, all those decades ago.

As a writer, I have often felt that the message in any story is best left ambiguous so that the reader can own the piece for themselves. The experience of reading is, after all, personal and, by default, subjective. However, in writing this author note, it has become clear that change is a constant concept in the chronology of how False Prophet came to be. So, if I had to distil the story down to its bloodied, beating heart, then I would have to say it is about duty and the the great burdens that come along with it, and—like the story itself—the nature of existential change. We all, at some point in our lives, yearn for adjustment and mostly it appears out of our hands, out of our control. False Prophet is about having the opportunity to be an agent of change. Like anything momentous, the costs of doing so are great. But it should never stop anyone from trying. Had this been the case, False Prophet would never exist as it does now. So, I leave you with a few thoughts. If we have the ability to alter events, should we do it without recourse? Does beneficent intention outweigh the potential for a cataclysmic outcome?

Food for thought? Time to tuck in.

Dave Jeffery
Worcestershire, UK, 2025

"Jeffery has a connoisseur's eye for the grotesque and mind-bending."—STEPHEN VOLK, writer of GHOSTWATCH and AFTERLIFE.

British Fantasy Award-nominated Dave Jeffery is the author of 18 novels, 3 collections, and numerous short stories. His Necropolis Rising series and yeti adventure Frostbite have both featured on the Amazon #1 bestseller list. Other work includes the critically acclaimed Beatrice Beecham supernatural mystery series for young adults, and the A Quiet Apocalypse series. His Campfire Chillers collection made the 2012 Edge Hill Prize long-list, and his screenwriting credits include award winning short films Ascension and Derelict. He is a long-time contributor to Phantasmagoria Magazine, a final reader for Space and Time Magazine, and a regular book reviewer for The British Fantasy Society. Prior to retirement in 2019, Jeffery worked for 35 years in the National Health Service (NHS), specialising in the field of mental health nursing and risk management. He holds a BSc (Hons) in Mental Health Studies and a Master of Science Degree in Health Studies. During this time, he has worked with Whurr International, Wiley & Sons, and the Royal College of Nursing's Mental Health Practice

Magazine, writing academic papers and research articles. Jeffery is also co-editor of Deafness and Challenging Behaviour (Wiley & Sons). His literary criticism has been published by Bloomsbury Academic and Peter Lang Publishing. Finding Jericho, Jeffery's contemporary mental health novel, has featured on both the BBC Health, and Independent Schools Entrance Examination Board's 'Recommended Reading' lists. He is a mentor on the Horror Writers Association's Mentorship Scheme, and the 2022 recipient of the HWA Mentor of the Year Award. For three years Jeffery was co-chair of the HWA Wellness Committee.

Website: www.davejefferyauthor.com
Instagram: www.instagram.com/davejefferyauthor
BLUESKY: bsky.app/profile/davebjeffery.bsky.social

EERIE RIVER PUBLISHING

NOVELS & COLLECTIONS
False Prophet: Dark Fiction Novel by Dave Jeffery (2025)
After: Horror Novel by Drew Starling (2024)
The Roots Run Deep: Collection by C.M. Forest (2024)
A Shadow Over Haven: Nick Holleran Series (2024)
Gulf: Dark Walker Series Book One (2023)
Breach: Dark Walker Series Book Two (2024)
Seed: Dark Walker Series Book Three (2025)
Chasing The Dragon: Horror Vigilante Novel (2023)
The Naughty Corner: Novella Collection (2023)
Shades Of Night: Night Order Series Book One (2022)
Untamed Night: Night Order Series Book Two (2023)
Dead Man Walking: Nick Holleran Series (2022)
Devil Walks in Blood: Nick Holleran Series (2022)
The Darkness In The Pines: Nick Holleran Series (2023)
The Void: Sapphic Fiction (2023)
They Are Cursed Like You: Trailer Park Witches Series (2023)
Infested: Horror Novel (2022)
SENTINEL: The Bensalem Files (2021)
NOTHUS: The Bensalem Files (2022)
Miracle Growth: A Cosmic Horror Novella (2022)
Helluland: Urban Fantasy of Legends (2023)
A Sword Named Sorrow: Fantasy Novel (2022)
Storming Area 51 (2019)

ANTHOLOGIES
The Earth Bleeds at Night: Anthology of Horror
Year of the Tarot: Four Book Series
AFTER: A Post-Apocalyptic Survivor Series
Elemental Cycle: Four Book Series
It Calls From Series (Forest, Sea, Sky, Doors, Veil)
Blood Sins: Shared World Horror Anthology
Last Stop: Shared World Horror Anthology
Of Fire and Stars: LGBTQIA+ Fantasy anthology
From Beyond the Threshold A Cosmic Horror Anthology

DRABBLE COLLECTIONS
Forgotten Ones: Drabbles of Myth and Legend
Dark Magic: Drabbles of Magic and Lore

COMING SOON
Infernal Night: Dark Walker Series Book Three (2025)
Order of the Rotting Goat: Horror Novella by Colt Skinner (2026)

AN EERIE RIVER PUBLISHING ANTHOLOGY
The Earth Bleeds At Night
EDITED BY HOLLEY CORNETTO

"GULF IS A HEARTBREAKING AND FRIGHTENING EXPLORATION OF ISOLATION, LONELINESS, AND TIMELESS CHILDHOOD HORROR."
—SUNY DEAN, AUTHOR OF THE BOOT KILLER

SHELLY CAMPBELL
GULF
DARK WALKER SERIES BOOK I

"GULF IS A HEARTBREAKING AND FRIGHTENING EXPLORATION OF ISOLATION, LONELINESS, AND TIMELESS CHILDHOOD HORROR."

INFESTED
C.M. FOREST